CROSSING FROM SHORE TO SHORE

A NOVEL

JEAN P. MOORE

RUNNING WILD

For my father

What is it, then, between us?
  What is the count of the scores or hundreds of years between us?
  Whatever it is, it avails not—distance avails not, and place avails not.

— WALT WHITMAN, "CROSSING
BROOKLYN FERRY"

CONTENTS

Naples, Italy
June 25, 1996

Walking along the bay, with Vesuvius in the distance, I see my shadow on ancient rocks, just as my ancestors must have once. Our shapes in shadows, evidence of our lives. I've come to Naples to feel closer to those now gone, no longer casting shadows anywhere on this earth. Their hometowns are nearby, where they lived as children before making the crossing, becoming Americans, and forgetting everything about their pasts, or trying to forget. Of course that is not possible. Their history is held in the blood of the children. And so we live our lives, this blood whispering to us, telling us things we hardly understand. And yet the stories will be told because until then there is no rest.

1

THE SHOEMAKER SINGING

New Britain, Connecticut
June 1914

H is new shop had not been opened more than fifteen minutes before a skinny young girl with long dark hair came bounding in.

My papà needs these fixed, she said. Her dialect was the same as his. He knew she was the daughter of Tonio Giordano from San Terma in Saviano, Erasmo's hometown.

The girl was fearless for her age. He could see that.

Permettimi, he said, taking the shoes up from the counter where she had placed them with a thud. He looked hard into her eyes and she did not look away. He told her the shoes would be ready in a week. His hand touched hers when he gave her the ticket. Her skin was soft and smooth, like a child's, but she was not a child. He told her that when she came back to pick up the shoes she should come by herself. He thought she might look away from him then, but she did not.

She left as quickly as she had come, but outside on the side-

1

walk, she paused. He could see her through his window. Did she stop there so he could look at her legs? She seemed to lift her skirt a little, or it may have been a breeze. He moved closer to the window to look. She lowered her head against the wind and pushed her hair back away from her face. Her hair, her blouse, her skirt, all blowing against her, leaving ripples in the fabric, like flowing water, like a river. He ran out to meet her, to say what, he didn't know, but she had already gone. He saw her running down the street, a little girl who wasn't a little girl who would be a woman soon. He would wait.

Back inside, Erasmo ran his hand over the wood counter. The texture, slightly rough, felt good against his skin. He had made it himself as he had the shelves and the hanging wood peg where his apron would go. Taking a deep breath, he let the nutty scent of the finish fill his lungs. Now all the woodworking tools would be returned to his cousin's friend who built furniture for wealthy families in New York City.

It had not been easy, saving money, borrowing from his cousin Cino, doing odd jobs for him, and sleeping on a cot in the backroom of Cino's tailor shop. Erasmo stuffed the American dollar bills he earned into the tin box he kept under the cot. Finally, he had enough money to rent the bottom floor from the German who owned the building and lived upstairs. One day, Erasmo thought, I will buy it all from him. And my wife and our children will live where he is now. Of course, Erasmo didn't have a wife or children, but he would.

Now he savored his labors. Behind the counter and shelves was an alcove where he kept his tools, his cobbler's bench, shoe forms and stands, his hammer and anvil and knife. Above it was a cabinet for his leather pieces and thread, soles, and heels; all had come at a dear price. And beside his bench, his prize: a new Singer machine for sewing leather. He had to beg Francesco in Brooklyn for the money.

Ciccio, he had said to his brother, why do you keep your success only to yourself? Don't you want us all to prosper, as you have?

This seemed to tug at him, and finally his brother lent Erasmo the money. Now Erasmo owed him, and he would pay him back. He didn't want his successful brother to have anything on him. Erasmo would be his own man.

Behind the alcove was a narrow opening to a small backroom, large enough for a cot, a four-drawer dresser, and to the side, a sink, washstand, and toilet. Erasmo had been able to get this space, with all the furnishings, from the German, without paying extra. The German was eager to rent to an industrious Italian who was starting a new business of his own. Everyone knew Erasmo had come to this country to make his mark. There was no gold in the streets, but a man could work for a living and see his chances improve.

This was his starting place. For now the small room and shop would do.

Was it only last year that he and his brother Giù made the crossing, as Ciccio had done before them, to start a new life? Even after the months had passed, this strange new land did not feel like home. True, there was the German, happy to rent to him, to take his money, and shopkeepers who surmised he would work hard and pay his bills. But there were others, strangers he passed on the streets. They shook their heads and muttered angrily in his direction, although he did nothing to arouse such disrespect. He may not have understood their words, but their meaning he knew full well. *You do not belong here. You are not our kind. Go back to where you belong.* Once, outside the butcher shop, as Erasmo opened the door to enter, a man in a suit passed him and spat just to the side of Erasmo's shoe. He let go of the door and turned to face the man, but he was already getting into a motorcar. In Saviano that man would be bleeding on the street. Erasmo pumped his hands open and closed but then unclenched his fists. No matter. This was home now, his and his brother's. He would have to be patient, show forbearance. Home. Erasmo missed his mother.

What would she think of her boys now?

You go there, and don't come back expecting me to feed you and wash your clothes, she said when they told her of their plans to leave. She put the tray holding four wine glasses on the kitchen table and put her hands on her hips. Then she just shook her head and picked up the tray to take outside for the customers in her garden. She had run the cantina out of their home for years. Their backyard had been the men's gathering place for as long as Erasmo could remember. There they would sit, drink his mother Nicoletta's wine, and talk. Those old enough to remember spoke of the Risorgimento. No matter their age, they all scoffed at the result. It was a lie, they said. As always, the rich prosper, and the poor suffer.

Let them talk, Erasmo thought. He would follow Ciccio to America. Giù would travel with him. Giovanni, the oldest, would stay. One day Gio, the first son, would own the house and the property and their father's tailor shop.

What is there for us to stay for? the two brothers asked. They worked for others. They had no wives, no children, and no property. Ciccio had left Marianna and his boys behind to make his way, and already he had a business of his own in America. Faced with this question, their father shrugged. He would not stop them. Everyone knew America offered what Italy could not, even if the streets were not paved with gold and even if the rich took from the poor there too. They did that everywhere.

4

On the day they left, Nicoletta packed food for them, salami and wine from the cantina, bread from the oven, and oranges from her trees. But she would not go with them to the train to Naples where they would board the ship that would take them away. She stood in the doorway and waved goodbye. Erasmo saw her turn, her shoulders rounded.

He knew she would never let them see her cry. The last thing he remembered about leaving that day was the scent of oranges from her trees.

* * *

By the time that first day, when Erasmo turned the sign from open to closed, he had five pairs of men's shoes to resole, three needing new heels, and one pair of women's shoes to be mended where the seam had come apart. The German had even left his rather large dress shoes to be polished.

Make a good shine, Erasmo, he had said, after congratulating him on a successful first day. You come to my apartment. I will give you a glass of wine from my country, white and sweet. You will like it.

They stumbled through English, eventually making themselves understood. Erasmo must turn down the gentle offer. He must see his cousin.

Guten Abend, then.

Buona sera.

In his backyard in Kensington, not far from New Britain, Cino too offered Erasmo wine, red, made by his wife, Felice. They sat under a large maple tree on a wooden table with benches on each side. It was summer and there was still enough sunlight for them to sit and discuss the day.

Cino raised his glass to Erasmo and congratulated him on opening his own shop.

But where is Giù? he asked.

Erasmo explained that his brother was in Brooklyn with Ciccio, where there was more room for him.

He has a small room and a bed there. He will come to live and to work with me when I have enough to buy a house, Erasmo explained.

Erasmo was proud to raise his glass to Cino's. Erasmo said in America it is possible to make money. It is better here than in Saviano. Cino nodded in agreement, but he also frowned.

There are some people I want you to meet, friends, he said. They are Italian, but not from home. Good people, amici. He paused then, as if struggling for what to say next. Something Erasmo might understand. They say we make money in America, but then ask, are we free?

But Erasmo was confused. Who were these friends, and what does that mean, *are we free?* Erasmo replied that he was free.

No, cousin. You are not. Maybe it is better here, but it is the same as in Italy. The government is for the rich. Workers have no rights. They are not free. And you will never be rich. They will let you mend their shoes, but they will never let you sit at their table.

These were not things Erasmo had thought about. He knew there was hatred. He had seen it and felt it, but he could hate too. There was equality in that.

I have no use for their table, he said. I just want to make enough money to have one of my own.

Cino shook his head. The day will come when you will understand. Come with me on Sunday to my friends' house. You will meet them and see for yourself.

Erasmo agreed to meet the Sanchinis', Cino's friends. The cousins drank wine until the sun was gone. Erasmo said goodbye and walked the two miles home.

* * *

The first Sunday he went there, to the Sanchinis', he saw her, Tonio Giordano's daughter. Erasmo pulled his cap off and held it in both hands as he looked at her. She was tall for her age, slim, and more womanly than he remembered. She moved gracefully, a fawn barely touching ground. She took a bite from a cookie she was holding and looked at him before smiling. She sat on the sofa in the apartment's meeting room, crossing her legs at the ankles. It was a move that seemed unfamiliar to her, as though she were practicing it for the first time. Erasmo thought of a young deer again, among flowers, but these were not real, only mimicked in the sofa's pattern. He wanted to walk with her in a field of real flowers. Her large brown eyes looked down as she brushed away a few stray crumbs that had fallen on her blouse, the same one she had worn when she came to his shop.

Irma and Giobbe Sanchini, a young couple, were setting out small glasses of wine and little fig cookies. Erasmo moved toward an empty chair across from the girl. The apartment on Mill Street was larger than Erasmo had expected. The Sanchinis' weren't much older than he was. They already had a front room large enough for them and for visitors. The woman was round, maybe a baby was coming. He could smell tomato sauce simmering. The scent of tomatoes, basil, and garlic reminded him of home. He thought again about having his own place, large enough for a wife, a baby, and a kitchen with sauce on the stove.

Cino introduced him to those assembled, to the Sanchinis', to Cino's friend Augusto and to Gabriella, another pretty young woman, who was with him.

And this, said Cino gesturing toward the girl on the sofa, is Amalia, the daughter of Tonio Giordano, from home.

Amalia, a nice name, said Erasmo, nodding to her.

Welcome to our group, said Irma. Not so many people today, but we meet on various days at various places, for whoever wants to come.

Keeping her attention on Erasmo, she smoothed her shirt behind her and sat on one of the folding chairs across from him. But when we are rehearsing for a play, we meet more regularly and there are more to join us. Amalia is one of our actresses and a very good singer, like a bird. So is Gabriella, she said, nodding toward each. Lia and Ella, our young songbirds, are important to our cause.

Erasmo did not know anything about a cause. He was confused. These were the friends Cino wanted him to meet, a couple in a gruppo who put on plays and sing. Erasmo was no stranger to gatherings of people who turned to song as the evening wore on. His mother and father sang duets in their backyard after the wine had been flowing. Erasmo was a singer himself on occasion. Always opera, always arias. His parents had gone to the Teatro San Carlo to hear *Tosca*. They could hardly afford the tickets. They had the worst seats, but you could hear from anywhere, his mother said. Nicoletta borrowed a dress. They stayed only one night in Naples, with cousins. For months after, the house hummed with various, detached lyrics. *Vissi d'arte, vissi d'amore, non feci mai male ad anima viva!* his mother sang. *O dolci baci, o languide carezze,* his father sang. He remembered clearly. What did playacting and singing have to do with the workers and freedom Cino had spoken of? No matter. Erasmo ate a fig and stared at Amalia.

As the afternoon wore on, the talk turned to a man of great power, at least according to Giobbe. He stood next to his wife and put a hand on her shoulder. He was not a large man. Slight and wiry, Erasmo thought, but there was strength in his lean

CROSSING FROM SHORE TO SHORE

and tan body. He told Erasmo, in this country, he was a bricklayer.

But I have been many places and have done many things, he added when he and Erasmo spoke after refilling their small glasses with wine.

There was to be no singing or playacting this afternoon. Instead, Giobbe began to talk of a man he called the best of us, but this man was not to be called their leader because they had no leaders.

No man is above any other, but this man is imponente, yes, an imposing man. And when he speaks, he commands attention. Because he speaks the truth. Giobbe paused to look around the room, to be sure everyone was listening, but Erasmo was sure Giobbe's focus was on him.

I have met him many times. When he comes to this city to speak to us, in a building big enough, people come from all over to hear him. He could have been a great lawyer, a rich man, but he chose to be a man of the people.

Cino, Augusto Segata, and Gabriella nodded and so did Amalia. They knew this man, too, or at least knew of him. It was impressive to be with people who knew someone so important. Erasmo wished Giù was with him. But he also knew it was easy to fall under the spell of an important man. His father had warned him to watch for false prophets. These usually included anyone who owned too much property, anyone in government, and priests.

Until now, Erasmo had been quiet, but without thinking too much, he asked, Who is this man who is strong but not your leader?

Giobbe looked at him and cocked his head to one side. Then he looked at Cino and frowned. Who have you brought with you today, comrade? Then back to Erasmo. I speak of

Luigi Galleani. Is it true you do not know of him? He looked at Cino again.

No, I don't know him, Erasmo said. But please, tell me. Why should I admire him? He turned toward the others. He looked at Amalia whose eyebrows were raised. Was she shocked that he didn't know the great man or that he was questioning his greatness?

Cino gave him a stern look but Giobbe smiled. Certamente, he said. It is our duty to share his name and the Beautiful Idea.

Erasmo listened as Giobbe spoke of this man's intelligence, his eloquence.

Everyone who hears him, applauds, even those who don't believe as he does. He is that powerful. And his words, we have his writings to teach us. Everything must belong to everybody, he tells us. 'To the poor must be given those things from the rich,' that is our belief. Even if we have to fight against those who would stop us.

Erasmo looked up, frowning. Giobbe, who most certainly was not accustomed to doubters, stopped speaking and shrugged abruptly, hands open at his side, questioning this nonbeliever in his midst. Erasmo cleared his throat.

Where I come from, those who could stop you, would. They always do, and they always win.

Erasmo had heard it all before. The state took from the poor to give to the state. Everyone knew it. The church took from the poor to give to the church, and the priests were never hungry, his father would point out. There had been revolts before, but it always ended as it began. The poor were never any better off.

Ah my friend, that is because in this fight you must be ready to give up everything for the Beautiful Idea, a world of perfect harmony and cooperation. In this world to come,

Giobbe went on, there would be no state, no government, no wars, no religion, no labor unions, no leaders.

Ah, Erasmo thought he understood now. These people were dreamers. Everyone would be equal. It would be naturally so. Everyone would work and everyone would share. Erasmo was not convinced.

This is what the priests speak of, the heaven that will come after the suffering, which of course the believers are told they must endure in this life.

No friend, said Giobbe, this beautiful idea is there for them in this life, but only after they rise up for it, after the revolution.

Giobbe continued his focus on Erasmo.

Let me ask you. You have been here for some months now. Do you see any difference here? People of means look down on the poor, on workers, on immigrants. There is no equality here —all men created equal—do you see that on the street?

Erasmo shook his head. It was true. There was injustice. There was inequality. He had seen it in the way shopkeepers spoke to the Germans and to the Italians, anyone from some-place else who couldn't speak English so well. He had seen it in how he had been treated. The angry words, the disrespect. He thought of the man who had spat on his shoes.

But, Erasmo said, I already have my business. I'm free to make a living here.

So you come with money they are willing to take and that is all that matters to you? The suffering around you is okay with you? Open your eyes, brother. See how your compatriots live, the squalor, the sick children, not enough to eat. And do they earn a living wage? Giobbe shook his head. It is intolerable, he said.

Erasmo was losing patience in the conversation. The lives of others were not his business, but he didn't say this.

Then Giobbe, this calm and gentle man, who with his wife

11

entertained guests and served wine in little glasses and handed out cookies, spoke of things Erasmo could not fathom.

It will take violence, he said, revolutionary violence. He became incensed and spoke of the war to come, in their towns, in the country, in the world. They would begin with the 'deed,' bombs against the enemy, the state and the borghesia, all those in their comfortable little lives, going to church, preaching love and charity, who never open their eyes, their hearts, or their purses, to the inequity and injustice around them. There will be bombs, there will be assassinations, more assassinations, he said, until the followers of the Beautiful Idea achieve the natural world we were all meant to have.

Hearing this, Erasmo rose. He looked around. Everyone in the room looked back at him. They had heard it before, he could see. Even young Amalia and Gabriella. The truth was Giobbe had stirred him. He didn't know what else to do. He sat back down.

When it was time to leave, Giobbe grabbed Erasmo and stuck a pamphlet under his arm. Read this, friend, he said. I'm glad you came. Let's see what you think the next time you come.

He shook Erasmo's hand and Cino's, and they said good-bye. Erasmo turned to see if Amalia was coming, too. But she stayed behind.

In his room that night, Erasmo pulled the light cord and lay on his cot, a pillow under his head, to read the pamphlet, *La Salute è in voi,* by Luigi Galleani.

2

I HEAR AMERICA SINGING

New Britain, Connecticut
June 8, 1995

A malia points an arthritic finger at a young woman in the photograph on her lap. "That's me," she says. "I was fifteen, but already... well, you see."

She holds up the picture for me. "You do look older—and very pretty," I say.

She smiles but lowers her head. "I was too pretty, maybe." She turns to place the photo inside the gilded frame back on the table beside the sofa where we are sitting.

"Wait," I say. "Please, who are the others?"

She turns again, with the frame still in her hands. She takes a deep breath, about to answer, and I take heart. She's willing to tell me more, maybe even what I've come in hopes of discovering.

* * *

This meeting has been a long time in the making, but I had only recently begun putting fragments of the story together at the state library in Hartford. There's a special room on the first floor housing directories going back to the turn of the century. I had reason to believe I would find listings for the years 1918 and 1919. And I was right. In 1918, Amalia wasn't listed, only heads of household were, but in 1919 she was, as "widow of Erasmo," the first I had seen mention of her husband. I knew the chances were slim that she would still be alive, but I continued the search that led me to this day.

My father knew all about the others in that photo. He knew what happened and more important, why it happened. I'm sure of that, but he never told me, not beyond one short conversation. And most of that had to be wrested from him. As though he held something precious and very private that was now being torn away.

When I was about to leave home to embark on a life of my own, my father decided to offer a shard of light into that past. I'm not sure why he chose that moment. Maybe it was a rite of passage he thought I was ready for. Or maybe it was because I was taking a job in Connecticut, far from our home in Florida.

Here's what he told me: "My family came to America like everyone in those days, because the streets were paved with gold. My papà's people were not peasants. In the old country, they were the craftsmen, *gli artigiani*. But they wanted more."

When my father talked about his boyhood and his family, when they were in Italy, it was with great affection. He described the sweet scent of orange trees in the backyard and family gatherings on warm evenings, men drinking wine and playing cards. From a young boy's vantage point, life was good, but the young men there had dreams of a new life far away, so my father would also tell about the time when his father and uncles came to America.

"My father," he would tell my sister and me, "loved his brothers, but he didn't settle where they did when they came over. He went to Brooklyn instead of to New Britain, Connecticut where his brothers went. They followed a rich cousin who had already made it big in America. But Papà did okay, too. With money he had saved, he opened his tailor shop. When he had made more money, he bought the shop and house that went with it. That's when he paid the passage to bring Mamma—your grandma, and me and my brother, your Uncle Tony—to the 'New World.'"

This much I had heard all my life. My father loved repeating the myth about the streets being paved with gold. He said it with much emphasis on *gold*. I realize now his animated telling and retelling was his way of expressing the great irony. No gold. Just hard work and resentment against immigrants. Then it was Italians. All newcomers had to go through it. He was resigned to this, a harsh truth as he saw it.

But this one time, he told only me more.

"My uncles, your great uncles, came to follow the cousin in Connecticut. This cousin was a tailor, too, and had his own home. And a family. One of my uncles wanted those things in America, but he didn't want to be in his older brother's shadow. That's why he went to Connecticut to get what he wanted: his own business as a shoemaker, a house above the store, and a beautiful, young wife. There would be room for a family. Plenty of room, even for the youngest brother.

"Everything was good for the brothers in Connecticut, but... maybe they tempted fate with their good fortune."

Here it seemed to me my father was getting close to another theme often repeated in his stories, of the *malocchio*, spoken of mostly as a family curse, never explaining, leaving us to wonder what terrible thing might be in store for us one day. My sister and I never took it very seriously, though. There were many things about our father that were different, that came with him from the old country.

And this story he was telling me now was about to take just such a turn.

"One night there was a party next door. A fight broke out. A man was killed."

My father looked at me to see if I was still paying attention.

I was.

"My uncles were accused of murder. And they were hanged for it."

Stunned, I waited for more, for some details, some explanation. But there was nothing. I, too, was silent for a time as these words took form. My grandpa's brothers were hanged. My only understanding of such a thing was from westerns on TV and in the movies. This did not happen to real people, to family. Then I asked for more.

"But how did it happen, why did it happen? Were they really fighting?" I assaulted him with questions. "How did the man die? When did this happen?"

He shrugged off my barrage and simply said, "It was a long time ago." He took a short pause. It had been a long time ago. He was only a child, still in Italy. He learned about it when grownups spoke of it in whispers in quiet rooms after the children were supposed to be asleep. "After that," he continued, "my father was never the same man. Our family was never the same. Papà blamed himself. He said he should have made sure his brothers came to be with him in Brooklyn, instead of going to be with the cousin in Connecticut. The big shot, with a car. Throwing his money around."

"Who was he, this cousin?" I asked. "What happened to him?"

But the time for more answers had passed. He looked at me as though seeing through me. "It doesn't matter. It's over."

And that was the end of the story. It seemed telling me this had taken everything he had. Shaking his head and almost under his breath, he said something I was to hear again, "Everyone said they were framed."

"Dad," I said, trying to get his attention. "Why would anyone go to the trouble of framing two immigrants who fixed shoes all day?"

No further explanation was forthcoming.

After my father died, the story of my great uncles haunted me. I couldn't forget the pain the event must have caused. To have grown up in a house burdened with such knowledge and then to have the story buried with the bodies, pretending it never happened, no one to speak of it? How hard that would be to bear.

I began to ask questions. My father's sister, Aunt Jo, wouldn't give up a word, except to repeat what my father had said, that the brothers had been framed. My mother put it another way. "Like Sacco and Vanzetti," she said. But by then she had Alzheimer's and at times, as if some plaques and tangles jiggled free, she would blurt out something perhaps meaningful but more often a brew of strange associations.

Finally, I let it go, the story of the doomed brothers—and the link it provided to my father. I had moved on, with a husband and a family of my own. The pull of the everyday can be a terrific force. There are carpools to organize, meetings to attend, shopping, cooking, a tsunami of distractions keeping us from facing essential truths. By burying the past along with the bodies, we do not eliminate the lingering questions that one day will emerge demanding answers. I was yet to learn this. I admit to feeling little empathy for my great uncles then. They were as distant as the most faraway star in the sky.

When my mother died, long after my father, I mourned my parents' passing but not their stories. I had given up on the past.

With the exception of mementos my sister Mary Ann and I had gathered, all else was bound for the trash heap, like the one she and I were piling high, going through their things before the sale of their Miami home.

We had attempted a similar exercise a few weeks after our father's funeral. But then our mother stood over our toils like a sentry, salvaging more than we could discard and returning old papers, documents, and files to the drawers where they had not seen daylight for decades.

With her gone now too, we returned to the task in what our parents came to call their office, a space in the back of the house where they conducted family business, as my father referred to it. That business involved my mother's skills and my father's oversight. He dictated the letters. She wrote them in her perfect cursive. He deposited his paychecks. She paid the bills and balanced the books, all managed with meticulous precision. She had been a secretary once for her brothers in their office in the Empire State Building, she often told us, sitting a little taller when she said it.

This space, once a large screened in porch, had been transformed years ago when our father enclosed it with sliding glass doors and added dark wood paneling, prompting Mary Ann and me to appropriate it as our hangout. Now, under the shelves that once held our record player and albums, there stood a large wooden desk and heavy matching chair, marking the slight but significant change from teenage rec room to empty-nester office.

We were on the floor next to the desk going through all the papers we had taken from the drawers. Mary Ann pulled a yellow sheet out of a file folder and began to read several names written in our mother's elegant hand. The names were followed by telephone numbers. Most we knew: aunts and uncles, friends, mostly dead. But there was one woman listed with our last name who was strange to us, Amalia Perretta. She had a Connecticut phone number.

"If Amalia on the list is a relative, she must be about Daddy's age, or something, so ..."

"Probably dead," I said, finishing her thought.

Even so, dead or alive, a family name from Connecticut was a lead, and that's how I was drawn back into our family's history.

Not long after, I called the number on my mother's list. I heard the three jarring tones and the announcement of a disconnected number, all to be expected.

I might simply have given up, but I was curious again. Who was she?

Some months later, I happened to mention the mystery to a friend who said family searches usually start with old telephone directories. She told me the best collection in Connecticut was in the library in Hartford.

Thus the visit to the state library where I found Amalia, "widow of Erasmo." But I also found her name, with a different address, in the most recent New Britain phone book.

At home that night I worked up some courage and dialed the number.

"I'm Amalia," the woman who answered said. After some confusion on my part, she realized that I wanted to speak to her mother. I feared the worst, already trying to formulate a new request, hoping that even the daughter might have answers to my questions, given that surely her mother was dead.

"Oh no, she's here. She lives here with me," she said, anticipating my reaction. But when I explained why I had called, she became more reserved. "She's frail. And she never talks about those times."

Perhaps I had said too much. There was more I had learned about Erasmo and his widow at the library that day, and now I had to be careful. Amalia's daughter was my link to learning more, and I didn't want to lose her.

"I see," I said. "And I understand, of course, but is there any chance I might talk to her just the same? I'll be careful."

There was a long pause. Then, "I'll ask. Give me your number. I'll call you back if she agrees, but she's old and I told you, not so well. She remembers everything. Her mind is good, but you will bring up painful memories."

Her words, abrupt, tumbled out in a torrent. She wanted to protect her elderly mother, it was clear. Although, she herself was in her mid to late seventies by my calculations.

"And I don't see the purpose. It's over and done, many years in the past. Why bring this up?"

Why indeed. Certainly, I'd given that very question a lot of thought, but until that moment, I'd never tried to put it into words.

"Because the past is never really done?" It wasn't a question, but I think I was asking for a connection, something she might feel too.

And for me it was true. The past was not done; it was a mystery. Maybe that was the reason for this pursuit, not just curiosity. Maybe it was because my father was often sullen, his father too. There was a deep-seated depression in the family that no one in those times put a name to. I just knew my father had had his share of dark days, and I didn't know why. And was there a reason, a reason that stretched back over the decades and was then handed down like a sealed box, with contents unknown, from generation to generation?

I tried to explain, this sense of unease, of something not right, something unknown. Maybe many families have this, a malaise of secrets, of things not discussed but present somehow.

She took my words in. I knew she was weighing their value.

I must have touched on something, that connection I had hoped for.

"It was forbidden to mention what happened. And they're gone now. My two brothers, dead. Their whole generation, gone, except for her. Only me, the others, cousins, scattered across the country. No one even in touch. When she's gone, it's over. Finally. Let the dead rest in peace. Isn't that right? We can't live in the past."

I heard her breathing, considering, before she continued, "I said I'd ask. I will. I just don't think ..."

I was losing her. Had I made things worse? A reluctant intermediary would not help my cause.

"You're right," I said. "It might be easier to let it go with her, but if the past is still there, in us somehow, maybe we owe it to ourselves to try, at least, to get at the truth." I was fumbling. "Does that make sense?"

She sighed, not so much in exasperation as in gentle assent. "Like I said, I'll ask. That much I can do. Besides, we're cousins, aren't we? But if she agrees to talk to you, don't upset her. Promise me that."

"I promise, and thank you," I said. "And we're first cousins, once removed." I heard her laugh softly before hanging up.

She called me back the next day. "She will see you. Come Thursday afternoon. And not for too long."

* * *

"That's Erasmo, my Ermo, to my left. He was much older," Amalia says, her attention again on the faded photo. I am tentative, but she seems eager to go on.

I searched the face in the photo for a long time, looking for a key to the man, and hardly believing there was now an image to go with the name. He was obviously older than she was, but still young. And strong looking, with a head of thick, dark hair. He appeared to be a man who would go after what he wanted.

"In a year we would be married—and I would be pregnant. So foolish in those days, so sure of love."

"Who else is in the picture? Next to Erasmo and next to you on the other end?"

Amalia runs her finger over the faces, landing on the one next to Erasmo. "This is Cino, their cousin. He was good to Ermo, gave him a place to live and lent him money to start his business. He was a good man. We all believed that."

The cousin, the one my father spoke of.

Amalia taps her finger on the image twice and shakes her head as if to shoo away a fly or an intrusive thought. And then she moves on to the young, slight man next to her. And I wonder how much more there is for her to tell me.

"That is Giù, Giuseppe, Ermo's brother. He came to make his fortune, and then to return home to Saviano, but he never made it back. You can see he is sickly can't you?"

So here was Giuseppe, the youngest brother. He did look ill in the photo. He was thin, and if I looked, I could see, drawn. More, almost skeletal.

"He had the coughing sickness." She looks at him and cocks her head and clicks her tongue. "Well, he probably wouldn't have lived long anyway."

Much is unspoken in that *anyway*.

I had begun to learn just how much more at the library that day, when I discovered not only old telephone books. There was also microfilm.

* * *

After locating boxes for the years 1918 and 1919, I settled down in front of the machine, threaded the microfilm, cranked the sclerotic device, and began to read the barely preserved, blurry, and cracked articles in the *New Britain Herald*.

That's when I learned that Erasmo and Giuseppe, my great uncles, were hanged for murder (just as my father had said) in Wethersfield, Connecticut on June 27, 1919.

The headline read: *Perrettas hanged at midnight hour*.

Reading on, my fingers and arms grew numb. Holding onto the knob that cranked the machine, it was as though I had enabled the dried ink to become liquid, allowing the words to travel through my veins and into my blood. Beneath the sensationalism, I caught a glimpse of the true horror my great uncles and their families had to endure. Regardless of guilt or innocence, setting that aside for the moment, here was suffering on a monumental scale. The men, women, and children whose images materialized were no longer vague figures from a dim past. Instead, I saw great uncles—young men—who would never see their children grow up, who would never see their dreams realized. I saw great aunts and cousins being deprived of husbands and fathers for a lifetime.

My eyes fell down the page to see notices of plays and picnics and ads proclaiming *The Bathing Season with all the keen enjoyment that accompanies it*. How isolated from the flow of American life as portrayed in the paper that summer were the lives and deaths of my great uncles, so far away from home, in America, the land of their dreams, where everything had gone so terribly wrong. They were no longer as far away as distant stars.

And then this, a jarring detail: *There were reports that Erasmo and Giuseppe Perretta were anarchists*. Was this true and why was it mentioned here, in this, a case of murder?

From that moment, I was desperate to find someone who might still be alive, who might shed some light on this tragedy. All this, so long ago, happened to a family living in New

Britain, my family. Maybe there was still someone in that city who could help. I tried the most current directory, and that's when, to my amazement, I found Amalia Perretta, the daughter, who led me to Amalia, her mother, and the widow of Erasmo.

And now I was here with her, to unlock the past. She began to tell me her story that afternoon.

* * *

I was a child, it is true, but many of us married at that age in those days. What was there to keep us at home? Chores, raising children, keeping men fed? I could do that in my own house, with my children and husband. So I saw Erasmo look at me. And I didn't look away.

I remember the day I walked into his store to drop off my father's dress shoes. The sole was coming apart. I placed them on the counter, looked up and looked right into his eyes.

He must have thought I was brazen to do that. Permettimi, let me, he said, looking back at me. He took the shoes into his hands and began to examine them.

Una settimana, he said, tearing off a ticket and giving it to me. He let his hand touch mine longer than he should have. 'You come back in one week,' he said. 'I will have them ready. But you must come back to pick them up. No one else. Capisci?' He smiled and then he returned to his work, so I picked up the ticket and walked out.

When I left, I knew he was looking out the window where he could see me, and my legs. I stopped to let him look, maybe I even lifted my skirt a little. I'm laughing now, but it was a stupid thing to do. If my father saw me, or any of my relatives, Maronn. That would be the end of me, parading around, letting a grown man look at me.

Do you know what he told me about that day? He said he thought of a river when he watched me leave, my long dark hair flowing, my skirt and blouse blowing against me in the wind. He could talk like that, like a poet.

He said he tore off his cobbler's apron as soon as he saw me stop. He knew I was letting him look. He quickly came outside, to follow, but I was scared and ran all the way home. From that day, he was after me, telling everyone he would marry me. It was a scandal because I was so young. My father did not approve. He didn't even let me go back to pick up his shoes. He wanted to look this shoemaker in the eye himself. He gave Ermo a hard time. 'Who are you to chase after my child?' he asked. 'What do you have to offer her?'

'I can wait,' Ermo told him. He said he already had a business and he could wait until he had a home for me. And when it came time for us to marry, a year later, Papà could not refuse. Because by then Ermo had not only his business, but his own home, soon to be our home.

From the beginning, Ermo and I were very close. He told me everything, and when we were apart, I could imagine his every thought. When we were together in the same bed at night, we dreamed the same dreams.

And that is how Amalia began her remembering. Each Thursday I would come and record her, and each afternoon she told me a little more.

3
VIENI O MAGGIO

New Britain, Connecticut
June 15, 1995

When I saw Ermo at the Sanchinis' the first time, I thought he was handsome. He had a head of beautiful dark hair and the most penetrating eyes. He had a habit of looking at you straight. Not just when he looked at a woman, which could have been too much. As if to let you know I like what I see, and I'll take it. Young men were like that in those days. Rough with women. No, it was a serious look. He wanted to know who you were, and he thought he could find out by looking into you, through your eyes. He did it with Giobbe, who was shocked that Ermo questioned him. He said after he left, that man wants answers, and he's not afraid to speak. That's good. That's good, he said again. He wasn't offended, not at all.

Ermo came again the following week. We were preparing a play for I Liberi, a group of people like us but who put on plays of emotion, with words and songs that moved people. My father knew Cino, who knew the Sanchinis. He knew I liked to sing and playact, so he asked Cino to send me to them. Irma said I would be good in the plays. Ella and I were the youngest and the prettiest and we both had good voices.

I should tell you more about Ella, Gabriella Antolini. Her story is very different from mine. When my family came to America, it was because my father thought he could do even better here than back in Saviano. And things for us were good there. But one day Papà came home and said, 'I have booked for us passage from Naples to America. We are going to the state of Connecticut where other paisani are, to be our friends in our new home.' We didn't argue, my mother and me. We went. And Aunt Abelia, too, my father's unmarried sister. It was okay, the move to America. I went to school and learned the language right away, not so easy for Mamma and Papà, but they got along. There were a lot of people, cousins or not, from home, like Papà said. We did all right. But for Ella and her family? A tragic story in many ways. They lost everything to come here because then, like now, there are always bad people to make a living off the dreams of others.

Ella's family came from Ferrara, in the North. Her father had a trade making and repairing wheels for horse wagons, but Ella's family was not so well off, so when a fast-talking crook came to their town with promises of making money in America, Ella's papà sold everything to go to this new place. He signed a contract for the whole family and followed this crook to a plantation in Louisiana. Ella told me she was eager to go because she was promised nice clothes to wear to school. This is what she wanted more than anything, not the clothes, but to be educated in America. What they found in the 'New world' was nothing but backbreaking work. A little girl, she picked cotton in the fields all day. They all did. She said it was like in the old days, before the American Civil

War. Only now they had Italians instead of enslaved Africans.

They made very little money to call their own, and what they made was spent in the company store for food. Home was a filthy shack. And, of course, there was no school and no nice clothes. There was nowhere to turn it seemed. They had signed a contract to be indentured servants and would be stuck there for years. The worst came when Ella's baby brother died from a sickness brought on by the terrible conditions. They wrapped him in her mother's shawl, the only one she had from home, and buried him in a field with nothing but a cross made of twigs to mark the spot, no priest, no prayers.

There were only two ways out from such horror. You could die or you could run. Just when the family thought death, like the baby's, would be their only escape, Ella's two brothers planned for the family to run. Miraculously, it worked. They were able to escape unseen by the foreman and guards (a miracle in itself, Ella said) and eventually they came by cattle car to New Britain where her father found work. But her mother was never right in her head again. It had all been too tragic. After losing every single thing they had in Italy, enduring those terrible conditions in the South, and after her baby's death, she gave up. That was the end of the dream for her.

But not so for Ella. She went to school and learned English quickly, like I did. She was very smart. She taught me plenty, like how it was our duty to fight against the corruption in America. She convinced me more than anyone that ordinary poor people lived in misery or died because those with money and power would do anything to keep it. She had lived this, had seen what neglect and cruelty did to people, to her own family, especially to her mother. She was the best anarchist among us.

She was devoted to our gruppo and worked hard on the

dramas, learning the songs and all the lines. We were both very good at it.

We were working on a play when Ermo came again. He seemed different. Giobbe had been sharing Galleani's pamphlets, *Cronaca Sovversiva*, with him. That's what they were, 'subversive,' because they contained the truth instead of lies, and that was subversive. Soon he subscribed himself, and his name was on the secret list Giobbe kept. He held up the latest pamphlet when he saw Giobbe and walked right over to him. I was afraid there would be trouble. He would argue with Giobbe if he didn't agree with something he had read. Sometimes Giobbe lost patience with him. I couldn't hear them, but then Giobbe kissed him on both cheeks. From then on Ermo joined us every week.

He had a wonderful voice. He sang tenor and knew all the Italian operas, but his best were Puccini arias, *La Boheme, Tosca*. For Italians, opera is like air. It is necessary for breathing. He learned our songs and sang in our plays. It was a happy time, a time when we began to know each other better.

In February of the year, that would be 1915, I turned sixteen. It was very cold, the ground deep in snow. Irma bought a bakery cake for me, a beautiful one, like my nonna made from a recipe her mother gave to her, a chocolate torta with almonds and sugar. Very fine and very delicious. I remember Ermo was there. He had a piece of the cake, and told me I looked very pretty. He behaved differently toward me. Like I was no longer a little girl.

It was winter but already we were thinking of Primo Maggio, a day as sacred to us as Easter. We would perform in the play of the name *Il Primo di Maggio* for I Liberi. Pietro Gori, who wrote the play, was our favorite, full of passion that made us yearn for a better world. He could spur an audience to action by showing terrible suffering under a brutal ruling class. It was so moving. I liked being in those plays.

On the day we were practicing, we started to sing, *Vieni o maggio t'aspettan le genti, ti salutano i liberi cuori, dolce Pasqua del lavoratori, vieni e splendi alla gloria del sol.* Isn't that something? I still remember. It makes me happy yet to sing. *Vieni o maggio.* Yes, we were all happy then. It was possible, the Beautiful Idea seemed possible to us then.

But I lose my thoughts. Ermo heard us, and he said, No, I know that song. Those are not the words. And then he sang, *Va, pensiero sull'ali dorate.* I don't remember the rest. But we had to explain. We were right. Gori took from Verdi to make our anthem. Erasmo learned the words, and from then on, he sang on Primo Maggio, the next year, the next, and the next. But that was all.

Did I tell you, 1915? That is the year we were married. Yes, after my sixteenth birthday, Ermo acted as if I was old enough for him to court me. After the May performance, I think it was June, he came to my house, cap in his hands, and asked my father if he could take me to the concert on Saturday. There was a park near our house and we could walk there. My father almost threw him out, but I said, Papà, it is okay. We will listen to music and come right home. My father knew I was capa tosta. And I was, very stubborn, and I would fight him if he didn't let me go, so he said yes.

It was a beautiful night under the stars. Ermo put his jacket down, and we sat on the grass. Listening to the band play marches and such. We both were offended when they started playing patriotic music, so we left. On the walk home Ermo, put his arm around me. He pulled me away from the path and behind a tree, he started to kiss me. I didn't stop him. I kissed him back. His hands began to roam to my breasts and under my skirt. Then I stopped him. It's okay, he said. I'm going to marry you. I laughed. And how will you do that? I asked. Will you take me to your little room behind the shop? Will we have our babies there? He was quiet then. He took me home and didn't ask me out again. I waited to hear from him but nothing. He ignored me at the Sanchinis'.

Later in the summer, he comes out of nowhere to my house and asks for my father again. This time he says he wants to marry me. I still can't believe he did that.

He told my father he had bought the building where his shop was and the apartment upstairs. I remember my father said to him, how did you manage that so fast? Mocking Ermo, like he didn't believe him. I thought Ermo would lose his temper and leave, but they kept talking. I heard my father tell him, finally, to go and come back when I was older. That was when I ran down the stairs and said, Papà, I don't want to wait. He was shocked, this I know, but he also knew me, what I was like when my mind was made up. Now my father knew for sure I would make life at home miserable for everybody, so he said yes. To tell you the truth, I was the one who was shocked. I never thought he would say yes.

Maybe I was a little uncertain about leaving home and mamma, but it was also true that in the two months when Ermo didn't come by, I kept thinking of his kisses behind the tree and how much I wanted him to touch me. I was sorry I stopped him. No, I wanted to marry him, without doubt.

And we did. My parents were furious that I didn't want to get married at the church. They said our marriage would not be recognized by God. I said it didn't matter as long as the marriage certificate was signed by the court. To tell you the truth, we didn't care about that either, about the state saying we were married. But we agreed at least to make our wedding legal in the state so my parents could sleep at night. As far as I was concerned, we were married the night of our kisses and Erasmo's roaming hands.

So the wedding was in August. My parents came to the courthouse, but no aunt or cousins, except for Cino. Of course Giù was there and Ciccio—Francesco. I was an outcast, excommunicated by the church. The priest told my parents that, but they came anyway, my mother crying the whole time.

The Sanchinis and our gruppo and actors from I Liberi made a reception for us at the big hall on Beaver Street. We didn't fill it, but everyone brought food and wine, and there was a band with dancing and singing, always singing. My parents didn't come.

And then we moved into Ermo's apartment. But first my mother and aunt went over and fixed it up for newlyweds. They put out fresh flowers and made the bed with new sheets. Mamma said the sheets they found on the bed were dirty. I knew what she was telling me, but I didn't say anything and neither did she. Her little girl was not a little girl anymore. My aunt left me orange oil to put in the basin to wash with. I never forgot that. She said the priest would be angry if he knew she was helping us, but she came anyway. She was very sweet, Aunt Abelia.

That first night, I can't tell you. It would make me arrossire, you know, blush from embarrassment. Women always said just accept what the man will do. You will not enjoy it, but it is your duty. That was not true. I felt everything he felt and more maybe. All night. What can I say? We were in love. There would never again be that love for me in all the years I would live without him.

4

THE HUNGRY AND THE RAGGED

New Britain, Connecticut
August 1916

She had stung him immeasurably. That is how Erasmo remembered it, when that girl, not yet a real woman, mocked him for not having a home to offer her. He had offered marriage, and she had laughed. He wouldn't see her after that. But he thought of her. The smell of her, the feel of her round breasts in his hands. He wanted more of her, but she had said no, even when he said he would marry her.

Everyone knew Erasmo was not a man to give up. He went to see the German. Look, he said, I want to buy my shop and the apartment above it.

That is good, Becker replied. But where am I to live, then?

Erasmo knew he was wrong to make such a demand, but he didn't know how else to say it. The English between them was a slippery thing, hard for each to grasp.

To Erasmo's surprise, a month to the day later Hermann Becker stepped into the shoemaker's shop.

I must go, he said. If you want to buy, it must be soon.

Without thinking, Erasmo agreed. Yes, he said.

Good, Becker replied. He named his price and said, cash.

They shook hands. Erasmo didn't have the money, not near the amount Becker demanded. Erasmo didn't try to negotiate. Something in Becker's tone revealed he was a man in a hurry.

Erasmo went to Cino, who said he would lend him half the amount. But you have a brother in Brooklyn, he said. Why do you come to me?

Erasmo went to Francesco. I will have room for Giù, he told him.

He hardly eats, said Francesco. He coughs. You may have doctor bills.

Francesco gave him the rest of the money, and Erasmo went back to the German, cash in hand.

The next day the German was gone, and Erasmo went to see Tonio Giordano. Back home, his family ran the produce store and owned the brickyard where other paisani worked. They may have owned too much, but they were not rich. No one in San Terma was. Erasmo had no quarrel with his family or with him, but how much would Erasmo have to endure to get this woman as his bride?

Tonio clenched his fists and said she was too young.

What is wrong with you? her father asked.

Erasmo told him he had everything to offer, a business and a home of his own. He was young and healthy.

Tonio shook his head. And how did you do that so fast? Or shouldn't I ask? The red in his neck rising to his cheeks. Go now. Come back when she's older.

Erasmo began to tense, preparing for blows, when Amalia appeared on the stairs.

What are you saying, Papà? Why must I stay here when I

can have a husband and a home of my own? You have Mamma. What do I have?

Erasmo looked at this girl who was a woman. She wanted him. Erasmo looked at Tonio, who had unclenched his fists, who seemed to lose height as his daughter spoke.

She ran down the stairs to stand at Erasmo's side. She was defiant. Tonio shook his head again and waved his hand at her. Capa tosta, he said, and turned his back as if to walk away.

Papà, she said, almost demanded. He turned to her again and said, What about school? You were smart in school, Lia. You said you wanted to stay and not work. I needed your help, but I let you stay.

She stood facing him, hands on her hips and answered. And what do they teach at that school? I'll tell you. Lies. Only their pretty lies. I will learn more reading on my own. I quit school anyway.

He stared at her, undone by her defiance. He turned to Erasmo. You want her? Take her. And then he walked away.

Erasmo remembered these events. How will a girl who speaks to her father in this way speak to her husband? Erasmo wondered what he was getting into, but then Amalia put her hand to his cheek. When? she asked him. And his fears fell from his shoulders and disappeared.

Standing there beside her, he said, Presto.

A week later they were married.

Now, a year after the wedding, in his shop he could hear the cries of Aldo from his apartment upstairs. Already three months old, his baby. Erasmo marveled at his good fortune. He heard Amalia's steps above him. He pictured Aldo on her hip as she stirred the sauce for his dinner. He could smell it, basil and tomatoes and garlic.

The German had left everything, much they had kept. Amalia discarded some and rearranged the rest. There was good silver, dishes, pots and pans. All these passed Amalia's inspection.

Why would he leave silver? she had asked. And the dishes, they are good china. He was a hunted man, she said. Change the locks, all the locks, and Erasmo did.

He complied with many of Amalia's wishes, no priests at the wedding or at the hospital when Aldo was born. No Sunday dinners for her mother and father. Aunt Abelia, yes, but she wouldn't come alone anyway.

Mamma and Papà didn't give us enough and would not come to our wedding party. Mamma, who listens to the priest, does not stop telling me I will burn in hell.

This seemed to be at the root of it, Erasmo concluded.

All Lia's pronouncements were fine with Erasmo, but he made a study of her demands. He didn't believe in beating a wife, but there might come a time, and he wanted her to know what might happen if she went too far.

But in the end, he was pleased with her. He had no reason to believe she would always want him. Wives tired of the bed, he had been told often enough. But not Amalia. From the beginning, from before the wedding, although they didn't have to wait long. He took her to see his apartment, and they made love on the bed before she had even washed the sheets left by the German. She was young and a virgin, but so wet, she did not scream out in pain, only in some cry of pleasure. She hung onto him until he was done. She was done, too, she told him. He was shocked by her. Was she normal? How would he be able to control her? What if she looked at other men?

One night in bed soon after the wedding, he looked at her in surprise when she wouldn't wait for him, fighting for her own pleasure.

When he finished, almost anticipating his thoughts, she turned to him, propped up on one elbow and asked, Why shouldn't I like what a man likes? Because I'm a woman? That's no reason.

He pulled her to him, and stroked her hair, but still he worried.

And so they made love each night. They made love and she got pregnant. And then they made love almost until Aldo was born. And now, even after the baby, she was eager for him to be in her. This was not something he could mention to his cousin or to his brothers. What would they make of such a woman? Of him?

He hung up his shoemaker's apron and climbed the stairs. Giuseppe was in his room sleeping, Aldo was in his cradle.

Would you like your dinner? she asked. Giù ate, a few bites, but more than yesterday. I think he feels a little better. He was tired, though, and went to bed.

She hugged him and he pulled away, almost afraid to arouse her. She looked at him, and cocked her head, but didn't say anything.

Maybe, she said after dinner, you don't have to be afraid to touch me. Maybe I want you because I love you.

Had he not considered this? He would think about it now.

Much had changed since that first Sunday at the Sanchinis' when Erasmo first thought of Amalia as a woman. He came to realize he shouldn't fear her ways that seemed unwomanly to him. She did not believe in the rules that usurped the right to be free. She was at the Sanchinis' apartment for more than the singing and the playacting. She was a good anarchist. She believed in the Beautiful Idea. And now he did too.

At first the words of Luigi Galleani stirred emotions Erasmo couldn't explain. He was angry. He was dismissive. He wanted what he knew he would work to have, a life in this, the country of possibilities. But the words leapt off the page. There was no denying their truth. No man should have to bow down to a master to have for himself what all men were equally entitled to. There would be no masters, no church, no government. These only kept men in servitude. It was true. Erasmo had seen the proof of it all his life. And it was true here, too.

There were long discussions with Giobbe, praise for him, Erasmo, who had come to be a believer and praise for his young wife who was brave and strong. More than once he had walked to his friend's apartment building on Mill Street to find him sitting outside smoking a cigar. Giobbe always went inside to get another chair and another cigar for Erasmo. Giobbe liked to quiz his newest convert, to see how much he had learned from his study. But from those hours sitting outside Giobbe's home, smoking his cigars, Erasmo grasped the real power of his study, the camaraderie of equals. This was the key to Erasmo's awakening.

Of course, the powerful are against us, Giobbe told his newest student. What would happen to their dominion over us if we woke up one day and realized we didn't need them? The simple truth is we know what we need and how to live our lives better than any of the forces now over us, better than the state and the church, better than the schools that teach us to doubt ourselves. What we don't know, we can learn and share, all equal. We just need faith in ourselves, to organize ourselves what needs organizing, and leave the rest, this need for hierarchy and control over others. How frightening this is to them. Who will work for the profits they reap? Who will give hard-earned wages to the priests who live like kings? Who will die in the wars of those greedy for more land? If there is fighting to be done, it must be done by us. We must be on the frontlines of our own liberation. This is our war, for our own freedom, which cannot be given but must be taken.

Erasmo had to grapple with these truths. He did believe they were truths. He had seen injustice his whole life. He always knew he had to fight for what he wanted and that if he was strong enough, it would be there for the taking, as he had done so far, crossed an ocean to work, to own property, to marry, to become a father. This was his dream and he had won it. What had changed? These evenings with Giobbe, his time with the gruppo, all showing him that it could work, that this other dream, the beautiful idea of freedom from oppression, was possible. What before he had seen as flimsy idealism now seemed real, in the hands of strong people willing to work and to sacrifice for the dream. When he sang the words of "Inno del primo maggio," something in him opened to possibility. *Come May, the people await you, free hearts greet you.*

And it was Lia. He could not deny her influence, her strength and her belief in the Beautiful Idea. When she told him Ella's heartbreaking story, the image of the baby wrapped in a shawl and buried in a field, he saw Aldo. That image became a small piece of the whole. He felt for the first time the damage done by the powerful few over the powerless many. Those odds had to change. He believed it now.

Giobbe told him, You and Lia will be a big help to us in the fight to come. We will be grateful to you. Luigi will be grateful to you. You must meet him.

Erasmo kept his feelings close, but this had caused his heart to jump. That he would meet the man who wrote so beautifully. He wanted this. And he was happy to be among these men who would change the world.

Lia, too, Erasmo said. She must meet him.

Giobbe laughed. Brother, it is not like that. Luigi will meet everyone, men and women, all who stand with him and shake his hand. She has met him, when he was here before. She doesn't let anyone turn her head. Except you, of course. No one is better than she is. She believes it. He is coming this Sunday night. He comes with little notice. It is better that way, not to arouse suspicion. Go home and tell her he is coming.

Erasmo knew he was not the same man who first came to the Sanchinis' apartment. These people, his wife, had changed him. He was proud to be among them and eager to do the work.

This time when he is here it will be different, Giobbe explained. We will not spread the word so much. Only those bound to the cause. We know who they are, twenty-five, thirty, maybe, from here and nearby towns, no more.

Galleani would come to the group's gathering place on Oak Street. He will speak first, then tell us what to expect, Giobbe said.

Things would be different from this day forward. Erasmo knew it.

* * *

When Eramso told Amalia about Galleani, she did not seem surprised, but she said something that made Erasmo take notice.

He doesn't come to such small groups anymore. Something is up. Giobbe knows, but he's not telling you.

Aldo woke from his nap with a piercing cry. Erasmo took him from his cradle and began walking him up and down the room. Being a father had not come easily. It had happened so quickly, but then what did he expect? Was he not eager for this, a wife and family in America? Maybe it was natural to be uncertain, so much responsibility. He looked into Aldo's eyes, tiny, but bright with rage, his cheeks red with discontent. Erasmo cradled and bounced his son in his arms, and the crying stopped. Erasmo lowered his head into the soft spot between chin and neck, heat rising up to meet his lips and nose. He breathed in the smell of sweat and recent milk. He thought again about the baby boy wrapped in a shawl and left buried in an unknown field.

Aldo began crying again. He's hungry, said Amalia coming in from the kitchen. Give him to me and go say hello to Giù.

His brother's room was dark except for dim light from the street that cast shadows on the wall behind the bed. Erasmo turned on the lamp atop the dresser. The light, still dim, revealed Giuseppe, propped up against two thin pillows.

He looked at Erasmo and smiled.

How are you, brother? Erasmo asked. I haven't seen you so much since you came from staying with Ciccio. Why were you sitting in the dark?

Giuseppe breathed in slowly, but still his cough stopped him.

I was taking a little sleep, that's all.

There is much to tell you, Giù.

Giuseppe didn't want his brother to worry or to call the doctor. He was tired and didn't want to explain all this. He leaned back into his pillows to listen as Erasmo told him about Giobbe's plans for Luigi Galleani. Giuseppe was not as interested in the dream, the plays, or the lectures as his brother was. He believed love had turned his brother's head and that Amalia was too young and too headstrong. The Sanchinis took her in and filled her up with talk of a beautiful future. How would this future arrive? Erasmo never believed such talk before.

But he kept these thoughts to himself. He had not been to the many meetings his brother had attended, it was true. These new compagni of Erasmo were interested in him only, it seemed. It was of no matter. Giuseppe wanted only to be strong so he could help Erasmo in the shop, even if it meant merely sweeping and cleaning up at the end of the day. At times his dream was of going home. America was a disappointment. He came down with the cough almost as soon as he walked off the boat, and nothing was as he had hoped when Erasmo first told him of all the opportunities in America. Giuseppe missed his mother. She would know how to make him well again.

Lia believes Galleani is coming for a reason, to lay out a plan. And that he will need our help, Erasmo told his brother.

Giuseppe nodded, as if he understood, but he understood nothing, and yet he would go to this meeting if that is what Erasmo wanted. He would stand by his brother. He wished he could talk to Ciccio, though. He would know what to do. He would talk sense into his brother. Giuseppe arched his back as he tried to take a deeper breath, but the effort caused his stomach to clutch. He knew he would cough again as soon as he let go.

The barren hall on Oak Street was used for bigger meetings, but the night Galleani came, chairs were arranged in a small cluster near the back, rows of six chairs. Erasmo counted five rows. There was a table by the exit door with coffee and several plain sweet cakes Amalia had made that afternoon to help Irma who, Amalia had said, was nervous and excitable.

She picked on me for little things, I was taking too long sifting the flour. 'There are egg shells in the batter,' she said. I took everything home to make in our kitchen. I've never seen her like that.

Now as the men were filing in, Irma greeted them. Her

smile was tight, her eyes, usually bright, were dulled with worry. Maybe Amalia had been right about her. She was not herself. Erasmo began to wonder what the night would bring. He was eager to meet the great man, but now a cloud had gathered, and his mind was not clear. Irma looked around the room. When her eyes met Erasmo's, she turned away quickly.

Other than the Sanchinis, Cino, Augusto, and Ella, Erasmo didn't know anyone, but he had seen the men with Cino, from Keningston, before. They were always hanging around Cino's place, sitting in the backyard, waiting for him to close his shop. Erasmo and Giù had met them when they sat and drank wine with Cino, when the talk always turned to politics and the hard conditions in the factories.

There were other men from neighboring towns Erasmo had never seen before. Three had come from Essex and two from Boston.

Giuseppe asked Erasmo why so many strangers had come.

They have come to hear what the great man has to say, he said. Something important.

Giuseppe shrugged his shoulders and took his seat in the back. Soon Erasmo and Amalia joined him.

Every seat was taken. Giobbe and Irma sat in the front. There was one chair facing the rows. It was for Galleani, but he stood behind it, his hands resting gently on the back. Erasmo took note of him. Not a big man, but alert, his eyes, behind frameless glasses, did not show anything but courage, as though he would be ready for any emergency. His brown suit looked worn, his beard trim. He could have been a doctor, a professor, or a lawyer, and in fact he was. Trained in the law early in his education, he never practiced. He left the profession to right injustice in another way.

Comrades, he began, I am happy to see you again. We have met before in large gatherings. Those have been essential, to spread the word, to welcome newcomers to our cause. Here he paused and looked from one to one another in the small audience. Erasmo, too, felt his gaze.

Galleani continued. But this group, few in number, has a purpose that is grand. We are one of many similar groups with a similar purpose spread across the country. Our method is to do our work without notice. So take heart in knowing that we are strong. There are many in many places who think as we do, who care as we do. Together, our numbers are as great as our cause.

He came around from the back of the chair and sat down, pulling it closer to the rows of those seated before him. He moved up on his chair, his hands active, slicing the air with each point. He seemed lightly balanced on the edge of the seat, as though he might take flight.

Our cause, you have heard me say many times, is to end the crushing oppression of the few on the many. We live, fight, and die, if we must, for the day when all men will be free to live in peace, the real peace, not the one the warmongers say they want. No, they want war to become bigger, to line their pockets. One day, when we win with the Beautiful Idea, we will all be working in harmony, all sharing in the bounty of the earth, not only the rich. And now the end for the oppressors is in sight. The chaos that is consuming Europe will soon spread across the ocean. After playing at war with Austria and Hungary, Italy will soon truly be in it, declaring war on Germany.

Here he paused, frowning as though from a great pain. Italy will be drenched in the blood of this senseless war, he said. And here, in America, we must be prepared, for our war.

He paused again as his audience murmured, some shifting in their chairs. Sensing this shift, Galleani's tone deepened, his words becoming more resolute.

Our war is not theirs. We participate in no war that takes up arms against the oppressed who die uselessly to aid their rich and power-hungry oppressors. Their war is the machine that fuels the powerful and kills the young and gullible. Our war is the quiet one, waged under their noses. We will strike when they sleep, and out of the chaos and destruction of their own making, a new world will emerge, a beautiful world of peace and freedom, and we will light the way. My brothers, we are at war, but it is our war, not theirs.

All the time Galleani was speaking, Amalia sat straight up in her chair, craning to see, nudging Erasmo, Why are we in the back? she asked him.

Erasmo, paying no attention to her, shot up to applaud at each stirring moment, just as others did. There was a rhythm to it, to the words and to the reaction of those gathered. All except Giuseppe. He listened. He listened intently. He thought of Italy in the war to fight the Germans. He wondered what he would do if he were home. He rose when Erasmo did, and clapped his hands as Erasmo did, but only to follow his brother. One thing he had concluded. This Galleani was a dangerous man.

5
O MIO BABBINO CARO

New Britain, Connecticut
June 22, 1995

D id I tell you last time about the babies coming? That started in May 1916, the year after we were married. Well, nine months later. I didn't care, but it was a good thing for my mother and father. Things at church were bad enough. What would the priest say, maybe during mass, if the baby came too soon? Everyone was still mad at us for marrying the way we did. But as far as Mamma was concerned, a baby was coming and there must be gifts. She would make sure of it.

After all the money I give every Sunday, be certain, they will give you gifts for Aldo, she said. But you have to have that baby baptized, or I will never give you another penny. And neither will anyone else.

I told her Aldo did not need to be baptized as far as we were concerned. You can imagine what happened next. We argued back and forth until she realized I was as firm in my beliefs as she was in hers.

Finally, I relented but told her Ermo and I would never set foot in that church. Mamma took Aldo to the priest herself. He was not even two months old. She demanded that he be baptized. She told the priest it doesn't matter what the parents do or have done. This baby is a new soul in the world. You must deliver this sacrament. It is your duty, she said. No one would come to his church anymore if he insisted that the parents confess their sins, repent, and receive the holy sacrament of marriage in the church. She said no, they will never agree, and if you refuse this child, no one will put money in the offering. We will go to another parish, she told him, and you will be alone here. That worked. The day was set.

Ermo and I were true to our word: we would not go. We dressed Aldo in his baptismal dress and gave him to my mother and father to take to the church. After he was baptized, they went back to my parents' for a party. We had no part in it. We did not believe in any god, not in priests, or in any religion. The way we saw it, the church fed off the poor and held hands with murderers, kings, or presidents. Look at history. It's true.

What's the use? Things never change. But then we were full of big ideas. I think of those happy days, when we were young and in love. We had our gruppo, picnics and plays, singing our songs, believing our dreams. Only for a little time. The world would soon go crazy again. Would the church tell boys not to march off to die in war? I never regretted not seeing Aldo baptized. I regret giving him to my mother and to the priest.

The following year I was pregnant again and happy a new baby was on the way. But the playing and singing were coming to an end. Believing our dream would one day be real? That took longer to end.

1917. If we had known what would come after . . . but how could we know? War talk was everywhere and hatred of immigrants, too. I remember there were fires started in early winter, big fires and a lot of damage. Our streets, immigrant streets, were full of state militia and local police. The papers blamed immigrants for all the trouble in the country. Enemy aliens, they called us. There was talk that we were trying to blow up their factories, the ones where they made weapons and supplies for the war. It was true, the factories were right here in New Britain. And there were more, in other places, big factories for war.

And Galleani had been right. In the spring we were in it. 'The Great War,' it was called. Galleani was arrested for some things he wrote. He said don't sign the papers for the draft. Ermo and Giù wouldn't sign up. Giù talked of going home. He said he would join the war there, but Ermo wouldn't hear such talk. Galleani himself said no to war, no to the draft. This war is evil, here or home, Ermo told his brother. Would you follow Mussolini, that puffed up idiot, or Wilson, who hates us? he asked.

Mussolini had changed his tune about conditions of the poor and rights for the workers. Instead, he started fearmongering his way to power, even then. A real pompous dictator in the making. Not many saw through him, but our people did.

I thought Ermo and Giù would fight each other over it, but Giù was weak. Ermo told him, Get better, brother. Then we'll talk. Ermo reminded him they had their own war to fight, and it was the real great war.

The truth is some of our gruppo were already doing the work of the dream. The fires? Cino, I'm certain, yes. Ermo and Giù? I'm not, I don't . . . . No.

What they did do, I'll tell you. Cino printed many copies of papers, telling men not to sign; don't be a dupe for the war. Don't sign for the draft. These were dropped all over town.

Ermo and Giù helped Cino do this thing. They did it more than once, print and scatter those copies from Cino's machine. It was all over the newspapers. They said it was enemy aliens because the English written down wasn't so good. A poor man, Russian maybe, was arrested, but not the brothers and their cousin. Why? One enemy alien was as good as another, I guess. Russian or Italian, it didn't matter.

The police maybe didn't know so much about us then. But we were being watched by other, more powerful people. This we were soon to learn.

Such a bad time. In the winter, my father died. My grief was so bad and how I cried. Ermo bought me a beautiful yellow handkerchief to wipe my eyes. But I put it away. My mother told me never give anyone a handkerchief for a gift because it will cause tears. A bad omen, she meant. I loved his gift. It was soft yellow, like butter, trimmed in lace, pizzo delicato. But, of course, I couldn't use it. Not then, anyway. I was already crying too much, and I had to stop because of the baby. I didn't want him to know his mother was so sad and that he wouldn't have a grandfather. He was too young for such news. So I put the beautiful handkerchief away.

My father was a good man, and I gave him so much heartache because I was so hardheaded. He always had to give in to me because I was too strong for him. Maybe I killed him. He was only fifty-one and he died of a heart attack. I was miserable with guilt, but maybe it was for the best. He didn't have to suffer like the rest of us, so much misery yet to come.

My mother was the first to see more suffering after Papà died, because of debt. My father always had money, or so we thought. When he died, the creditors came. They waited a little while, until he was buried. But then they came, hat in hand, sorry to bother the widow. He owed everyone, it seemed. The worst was the bank. We found out Papà had a mortgage. Mamma didn't know either, but he was behind on making payments. In a few months, they took the house. And my mother had to move in with my zia Abelia.

Papà always took care of his sister. He was sorry she never married. There was a man once, but he turned out to be no good. He promised to marry her, but he was a drunk and a thief. One day he disappeared, but first he took my zia's gold bracelet, the one my nonna gave her when Mamma and Papà got married. It was to make her feel better because her brother was getting married and she wasn't. I think Papà felt guilty that things worked out for him, but not for her, his only sister. In this country, when she came with us, he made sure she had her own apartment. She took in piecework to help support herself. She was good with a needle, so she helped a tailor Papà knew. In those days, that's what a lot of women did. But Papà always gave her extra money. So when my mother had no place to go, of course she went to live with Abelia. She was like a second mother to me.

When all this was happening, I was pregnant, with my big belly, but I went to help Mamma move. She sold most of her furniture and gave some to us. Ermo and Giù helped us move her, too. I was carrying some heavy boxes up the stairs when Cora Necchi stopped me on the landing. She lived next door to us on Cherry Street, and had come here to see my mother. Then she said she wouldn't let me pass because my mother owed money to her brother, Frank. Her brother? He was a fish peddler. How could my mother owe him money? She never bought his fish.

My father, he owed the money, for a loan, Cora said.

What loan? My father didn't need money from a fish peddler.

My father, she said, owed everyone money. That was why

you are here, moving your mother into a small apartment. She didn't even get to keep her house, she said.

So I put the boxes down. I pushed her. And she pushed me back, and I began to fall. I caught myself on the way down by reaching for the banister. Next thing, Ermo comes out of the apartment, comes down to us, and is grabbing Cora.

What have you done? He yells at her, and grabs her by the hair. At the bottom of the stairs is Frank. He yells up to Erasmo. Lasciala da sola, he yells. Leave her alone, or I'll kill you.

Erasmo begins to rush down the stairs. By now I'm standing, and I run down to stop him. I get in front so he can't go to Frank.

I'll get you, Palmese, he yells over me. I won't forget.

I tell him to go inside. He wants to know if I'm all right, and I say yes. He smooths my hair, and we go up to where my mother is standing behind the open door. She motions us in.

She tells us to sit and brings me a glass of water. When she is sure I'm okay, she tells us it was true, that my father had borrowed money from Frank. She found the note in his pocket when she was folding and packing his clothes to take to the church. Aunt Abelia joins us and says it's true. It was hard for her to say. She idolized Papà. It made sense to me then, how Papà let me go. He owed money, and Ermo had a place for me.

The next day, I started to bleed. The doctor said go to bed, so I did.

Ermo went to Cora next door. He yelled at her and said it would be her fault if anything happened to me or to the baby. And he shoved an envelope of money at her and said give it to Frank.

If Lia or the baby suffers from what you did, you and your brother will hear from me, he said. And that was the end of it. Or it should have been the end of it. But everything got so much worse later. I don't want to talk about that now.

Two happy things in 1917. Our second bambino. A few months after the bleeding, which stopped, Nino was born. We named him Nino. That is what we called him, but his name was Benigno. We hoped his sweet innocence would protect him, then and always . . . We were so happy. Another boy, another son for Ermo. He was a good father. How he loved his family. Remembering those days? Those are the good memories.

And the last thing I want to tell you is how the year ended. Tragically, beautifully. It's true. Life is hard, but you must accept the good and the bad. First, the bad. By the end of the year, we were in trouble.

The authorities were after us, the ones from Washington and the governor's people too. They were all after us, the followers of Galleani. Terrible things were happening all over the country. Our people in other states were put in jail. Mothers were separated from their babies and sent to prison. Their children were taken from them, and no one knew where they were. This was done even though there was family to take care of them, grandmothers or aunts who wanted the children to stay with the family.

We mothers were true comrades, but we could only go so far. We were strong. We wanted to fight for the Beautiful Idea, but it was true, the price was too high. A woman in jail could not be a mother. Women without children were better.

But all of us, men and women, had to be careful. We were under the gun. No more announcing our meetings. No, we had to change our locations from day to day, and keep secrets about where we met. So much of this story is sad. But the night of the snow was meravigliosa, a truly marvelous night I will never forget.

We met in an old, closed factory. Cino got the key from a friend of the owner. We spread the word among our group. We would have our New Year's Eve party as always, and we would have a speaker, Raffaele Schiavina. He was not as good as Galleani, but he was good, and we wanted to hear him. He was to tell us about our war and how to be careful because there was more danger coming. Many things were happening all over the country. Italian anarchists, they called us, the government and the newspapers. It was bad. Italians who had nothing to do with us were cursed in the streets, Germans, too. Ermo's German was arrested, we found out later. I knew he was in big trouble, by the things he left in our apartment. And Cino would be spied on, him and the men who were always at his shop. He and Irma and Giobbe would be in trouble, too. And beautiful, young Ella, my sister in our struggles. So much heartache was coming.

But now I want to tell you about our party, when it was very cold. We wore our heavy coats over our fancy clothes. We drank and gave our speeches and called out our slogans, *contro la Guerra, contro la pace, per la rivoluzione sociale.* And we laughed and raised our glasses to one another. We still believed in our beautiful futures.

Outside the weather got worse. It was a blizzard, I tell you. Schiavina never made it. His train was stuck on the tracks we found out. So we drank more wine and sang more songs. Soon everyone wanted to hear opera, and they wanted Ermo to sing.

He pulled me up from my chair and we sang the famous duets he learned from his mother and father—and that he had taught me. I still remember the words, *Al tuo fato unisco il mio, son tuo sposo,* Ermo sang. Then me, *E tua son io.* Ermo had a beautiful voice. *Tramontate, stelle! All'alba vincerò! Vincerò! Vincerò!* Do you know this? It's beautiful, isn't it? Oh how they cheered for us. I covered my eyes, I was so embarrassed. But Ermo? No. He bowed and took in all the praise. When everyone went back to their wine and their talk, Ermo took my hand and led me out to a little balcony. For one moment only, the snow stopped and the sky was clear. There was a star above us. He held me to him. We kissed before the star was gone. A big wind came. I shook from the cold, and we went back inside, locking the door behind us. Inside it was the new year. I can't remember a time when we were happier.

6
LA SALUTE È IN VOI!

New Britain, Connecticut
December 1917

I t had been a year Erasmo never could have imagined. At the beginning of it, he had everything he came to America for: a family, a home, and a shoemaker's shop of his own. But then with the war in Europe, even that far away, everything changed. Soon he could see what else was coming. He knew why Becker had sold him his building so quickly. He told Erasmo he must leave and had no time to bargain. When Erasmo asked why, he said, They think I am a spy. I am a foreigner. That is enough for them. For who? Erasmo wanted to know. The government, the people who have power, Becker told him. But they didn't have the words between them to say more.

Becker got as far as Bayonne, New Jersey. Then almost a year later there were the explosions, *devastanti*, of war munitions, millions of pounds of it, at Black Tom Island in New York Harbor. It was devastating. The sounds it made could be heard as far as Connecticut. Windows were blown away, babies knocked from their cribs, and people killed. War munitions, headed for war in Europe and set off in America. Who could have done such a thing? It wasn't the Italians, not this time, Erasmo knew. His knowledge of German immigrants and German spies was next to nothing, but he heard from Cino, who knew such things, that Becker had been arrested. He might hang, but there was no evidence against him, Cino said. He was with friends, not even in New Jersey, when it happened. Becker meant nothing to Erasmo, but this news shook him. The man whose property was now his . . . it made him uneasy to think he might hang. The times were getting dangerous for Germans and Italians, for any immigrants. This country didn't like the strangers who lived among them. That was certain.

And yet there was the work that must be done. Erasmo could not turn away from it. He was not a violent man. He did not believe in war. He did not believe in violence or assassinations or bombings. But what was a man to do when the powerful were violent against the powerless? Was it just for rich owners to starve their employees by making them work long hours for a meager wage, by giving only poor and dangerous conditions in return? And when workers wanted more money and better ways to work, was it just for the police to beat them brutally and then to say it was up to the police to stop unrest in order to maintain the peace, when it was they who caused the unrest? Was it all right to treat newcomers to this country like criminals, to throw them in jail, like Becker, to kill them without evidence? Was that justice? These were the questions he had come to ask in his new country. The answers were discomforting. So violence would be met with violence until the revolution was won. This is what he came to believe.

Because he was stirred by the words of Luigi Galleani, his

heart beat fast when he met him at the hall on Oak Street. When Amalia and Erasmo shook the great man's hand, Amalia was calm, as Giobbe had said she would be, but his own hand was damp, giving away his nerves. Amalia soon walked from them to be with Irma who was talking to Ella. Irma looked toward Giobbe and nodded her head but did not look at Erasmo.

Galleani told Erasmo he had heard much about him and that he would have work for him soon. Erasmo wanted to say something that would impress the man. He had read every word and was an ally to the cause, but the words wouldn't come, and all he could do was hold onto his hand. Finally, he managed to say he would do whatever was necessary. Galleani looked him directly in the eye. His grip on Erasmo's hand grew firmer. Galleani nodded his approval, released his grasp, and turned to talk to others.

The day after the meeting, Cino came to see Erasmo in his shop before he closed. Cousin, he said, I am glad you are here. I want to talk to you alone.

He and Erasmo went into the back room and sat at two stools facing each other. Luigi has a job for me and wants you to help. He knows, and Giobbe, of course, that I will ask you, but just you, not your brother.

Erasmo listened to Cino. So it was starting He would keep his promise to Galleani to work for the cause.

And don't talk about this with anyone, Cino added. Not even Lia.

Erasmo asked why not Lia? She is the strongest among us, he said. But Cino would not change his mind.

Listen, he said, if she gets involved, it will be bad for her and for your family. The less she knows, the less she can be forced to tell. Believe me, it is better this way.

Erasmo nodded. For Lia and for his family, he would

accept this, but already he felt adrift without her strength to help him.

We will begin to stir the pot, no? said Cino. Not like Black Tom's, not that big, not yet, but soon all across the country, we will make our presence known.

Erasmo knew things were brewing, that war talk was everywhere, but he was not sure what they could do to stop it.

Cino must have sensed Erasmo's doubts. The Americans are revving the war machine's engine, and we will let them know they have another war to fight.

This puzzled Erasmo who wanted to know why they should take such a risk. How can we fight them if we are caught?

Was Cino growing impatient? It was hard to tell.

This is your chance, Cousin, to show you have the strength to fight. Revolution cannot hide in the shadows forever. But, he added, we won't be caught. We are smart, the way a little mouse escapes the cat. Then Cino told him what must be done.

The February fires, seven, caused a lot of damage. There were factories in town that made parts for guns, that made grenades for war. More factories would soon be converted to make weapons and ammunition. Erasmo and Cino looked for buildings nearby that would burn, not the factories for war, but other buildings, to send a message. The game of cat and mouse was beginning.

The buildings that looked right were those that had been abandoned. The cousins looked for broken glass, for broken basement windows. They looked for trash piles. They looked for what would burn. What would cause a terrible blaze. They searched during the day, walking the streets, careful not to draw attention. They began filling cans with gasoline, going in Cino's motorcar to different towns. They tore rags into just the right size. They collected bottles just the right size for the rags. Then they waited for a dry winter night.

The February night of the fires was dark. No moon shone on two cousins driving a motorcar with no lights onto the streets where the old buildings were, where the factories were nearby.

Quickly, street after street, Cino drove the car to the chosen destinations, and with the motor running, Erasmo jumped out with cans of gasoline. He doused the trash, he threw bottles with rags and burning wicks through broken windows into debris-filled basements. They did this one street after another, until a conflagration arose. They saw the dark winter night turn bright orange as they sped away toward home.

It wasn't long before the clanging of gongs and ringing of bells broke the silence of the night. People in coats and under blankets filled the streets to watch the orange flames.

Amalia had told Erasmo to get out of his clothes as soon as he walked in the door. You smell of gasoline, she told him.

He had not said a word to her, as Cino had ordered. Did she know? What did it matter? She would do what had to be done. Besides, a wife would not be expected to testify against a husband.

As the night passed, the streets where the immigrants lived were filled with policemen and the state militia. They were called in to keep the peace on peaceful streets filled with puzzled residents, not flame-throwing anarchists. Those were in their beds, not asleep, but with good alibis.

The governor may have been preparing for war, may have been collecting information about men and materials ready for war, but not everyone was compliant. Not every man would fight the rich man's war. Not every factory making bombs would escape the anarchists' pledge of the 'poof,' of the explosion that would be caused by those who would make bombs of their own. The mouse had sent a message to the cat.

It was done and done well. They escaped blame. Luigi was pleased. The Sanchinis were pleased. We must keep the temperature to a low simmer, Giobbe told Cino. There will be more orders to follow.

Erasmo put on a brave face, but the fires left him shaken. It was not easy to see such destruction and to know you did it. No one was killed or even injured, but the chance was there. Innocent people will die, Cino told him. It happens. Just as the innocent women and children die in all wars. It is unfortunate, but it will happen. This did not ease Erasmo, but he did not show it. And there was Lia. She was stronger in her beliefs than he was, but he couldn't tell her. If he could, he knew what she would say. He could hear her. Do you want our children to grow up in this unjust world, or do you want them to be free, truly free, in a world with no more wars? Then we must fight this one for them.

* * *

Lia. This was the year her father died. A man sat on the side of his bed and bent to tie his shoes. Next he was on the floor for his wife to find, his eyes blank, as they must be in that moment between this life and another. Poor Lia, learning the truth, this man, her father, had left the family penniless. Her mother, losing everything and moving in with her dead husband's sister in a small apartment. Erasmo remembered going to Tonio for Lia's hand. Erasmo had wondered if he was doing the right thing, taking her from such a beautiful house. But it was for the best. Where would she have gone if he, Erasmo, had not provided for her?

Thinking about the day Cora almost pushed his pregnant wife down the stairs made Erasmo's heart pound, even now, after months had passed. If Lia hadn't stopped him, he might have killed her, he was that enraged. Not a violent man, but there was a limit to what a man could take. These things still troubled Erasmo.

* * *

All during the year he had worried about Cino but could not tell his wife. After the fires, his cousin was often with the Sanchinis, who were never out of touch with Galleani. Messages were sent and received with ease. He had seen this himself at Cino's shop, people coming to the door to drop off word and to take messages away to the next delivery point. All across the country it worked this way. Cino told him many things but not everything. Erasmo knew there were limits.

By April, the mouse was ready for more toying with the cat, but the game would change, although none of them knew then by how much. War was declared. America was in it. In May, Galleani published "Matricolati!" Here was written resistance to the draft and the government. In June, not long after Nino was born, Cino came to Erasmo with another plan. This time, he said, you can include Giù, but, he said, leave Lia out of it. This time Erasmo might listen to Cino with a deaf ear.

Lia wanted action more than anyone. She grew red with rage each time she saw posters of what she said was Wilson's war machine. One day when she came back from shopping, she left the bags on the kitchen table and saw that Erasmo was lying down in their bed.

You rest while the world is going to hell? she said, throwing her hat on the bed by his feet. She never did this, leave a hat on the bed, because, she had told him, it is bad luck. He watched her pick it up and put it on the dresser.

Strange, this wife, he thought. She will not step foot in a church because the priests are hypocrites and spread terrible lies. And these lies, she said, were superstitions the priests used to prey upon the ignorant. And yet here she was, removing a hat from the bed because it was bad luck. Bad luck. He knew that was what she feared most. So much of life could not be helped—a father dead of a heart attack no one could have predicted. Was it God who did this, or just bad luck?

Maronn, ridicolo, she said. They think we are stupid? Who believes this folly? 'Be one hundred percent American, sign up,' one poster says. And another one, 'America let you in; now you must serve her.' Follia. Men sign up because they see a picture of a pretty woman? Follia.

Tomorrow they must sign up, Erasmo affirmed, sitting up now. It was true. Registration was tomorrow, and all able-bodied men must sign. Even immigrants were expected to do it.

But you won't and Giù won't, she answered, sitting next to him on the bed. We must do something.

Yes, we must do something. And so he told her.

That morning, Erasmo had been with Cino. Felice and the children were at mass. She goes without me, Cino had said. What she believed, he didn't know. The two men didn't talk about it further. There was more important business to attend to.

Hundreds—thousands—of papers were printed in Cino's shop, in the back where no one could see. But the smell of the ink from the big machine was difficult to hide, so Cino opened the back door to let in the air. He looked left, then right, to be sure no one was watching.

Tonight, we will cover the entire city with these pages from

Cino's machine, Erasmo told his wife. He knew what was coming next.

I must come, too, she said, pacing in the room. I must help. I will leave the boys with my mother and Abelia.

She was busy making her plans when Erasmo reached for her from the bed, grabbing her arm.

Lia, listen to me. I'm sorry, but you cannot help.

He knew she would curse him and Cino. He knew she would fight this. Her strength threatened to overtake him. He grabbed her by her shoulders and raised his hand to her. She stopped then, but with her eyes she dared him to strike her. And he did not.

You must listen to me, Lia. It is not my decision. It isn't even Cino's. It is Luigi himself.

Amalia cried at this. Was it a game, were they not all equal, men and women alike? Her temper rose again. She would curse them all, these hypocrites. Men. She was stronger than all of them. She could do what any of them could do. Erasmo was at a loss.

He tried again to calm her, but what would he say? There will be a time for you, I promise.

You promise? You? And who are you to make such a promise?

Erasmo let her go. The babies began crying from their beds, and she would go to them.

It is because of them, isn't it? she called to him. And it was true. There were limits, even in the gruppo. If mothers were jailed, or worse, faced long prison terms, what would become of the children?

Erasmo watched her take Nino from his crib. She looked to Erasmo standing in the doorway, her eyes no longer bright with rage. He watched as her shoulders lowered. Nino was calm at her breast, but she was not calm. This was something else. Her eyes were fixed beyond him now. He couldn't know what she saw.

In the darkest hours of the night, the work went as planned. All over New Britain, Cino, Giuseppe, and Erasmo, carried their papers in big sacks. They climbed up on roofs and threw armfuls at a time over the edge, the pages flying in the wind like pigeons carrying their most important messages: 'Don't be fooled,' 'Don't fight the rich man's war,' and 'Don't sign up to kill men as poor as you in a foreign land.'

Cino, whose English was better than Erasmo's, had written these words. They now lay strewn everywhere: in front of the barbershop, on the sidewalks, and pressed against the doors of the grocer's. They lay scattered on the steps of the newspaper office and in front of City Hall. They found their way from the entranceway of the diner, to the park, around the monument, and under the wings of victory. From Arch to Main, every street was flooded. After climbing down from the last roof, still undetected, they nailed the remaining sheets to the doors of the shops and buildings they passed.

Home safe and in their beds again after this deed, their work was done until the next call came.

The day after the official draft registration had begun, Erasmo closed his shop early and walked to Kensington. He sat with Cino under the big maple while his cousin read the bold headlines that signaled the story: 'Anti-draft Radicals Among Us' and 'Our Streets Blanketed with Anti-war Propaganda.'

Cino continued aloud. When he finished, the cousins were relieved. No one had tied the story to the anarchists among them. Not the newspapers or the police.

Poor man, Cino said to Erasmo, when he read of the Lithuanian immigrant who had been arrested for what they themselves had done. They don't know who did it. That is in our favor, he said. But others more powerful are watching us.

Strangers asking questions. We must be very careful. Our luck will not hold out forever. He closed the paper with an anxious snap, but Erasmo knew that for the time being, they had done good work.

Lia knew it too, but she had changed, Erasmo could see when he returned home.

So the men have done a job any woman could have done just as well, she said. She had been folding diapers into neat piles on the kitchen table, but she stopped and thrust the few in her hand into Erasmo's arms. You put them away. She walked into their room and slammed the door behind her.

Erasmo was in no mood to go to her. He put the diapers on the table. He paced. This was not to be tolerated. A woman does not treat her husband in this way. The more he paced the angrier he became. Behind the door, she must have heard him pacing and become angry because minutes later, she opened the door and lashed out at him.

Long before you came with your questions and your doubts, I was a good comrade at the Sanchinis'.

Erasmo stopped pacing. She tried his patience to the breaking point. Any man would see that, but now he listened.

I did not ask questions, she continued. Mine had already been answered. I had read and studied and attended meetings. I listened with a full heart. But you come and suddenly you're the one to work while I stay home and tend to babies. 'All are equal here, men and women,' that's what they said, but it was lies. Just like everything else when men are in charge. Lies.

Erasmo could see that the very words she spoke meant she could not cry. She held her breath and her lips tightly closed as if to build a barrier to her tears. He let go of his anger and took a step toward her, but something told him she was not ready for his embrace.

* * *

They escaped suspicion after the deluge of paper, but as time went on, it was no longer so easy to escape watchful eyes. Things were soon to turn.

On a warm and promising day later in June, Cino quickly entered Erasmo's shop and closed the door behind him, turning the hanging sign from open to closed.

Our great man has been arrested. These words sank into Erasmo's heart as though a knife had been plunged there. Of course he was alarmed for the fate of his leader, although he was not to be called leader, and yet he was. But perhaps without fully grasping this feeling, this alarm, realizing, yes, it was for the great man, and yes for Cino and his comrades, but mainly, and now he had to admit, mainly, the alarm was for himself, for Lia and his boys. Fear ran through him, edging out alarm.

How is this possible? Erasmo asked. He is safe, always safe. Nothing traced back to him. Is this not so?

It doesn't matter. Everything traces back to him. He is Galleani, and maybe ...

And maybe?

And, yes, maybe to us. That is possible. He began pacing. He glanced up at the shade covering the window and pulled it down. We must be very careful. No one has suspected us, the fires, the leaflets. No one is coming for us. We have been unseen in our own neighborhoods in a town that doesn't know us. They do not understand us or our language. That has been useful, but perhaps there comes an end to being unseen.

Cino continued, each new detail more unsettling than the last. Galleani was arrested for publishing his pamphlets. There was a new law that made him a suspect. His *Cronoca* was anti-war and anti-American, the authorities said. It preached an end to capitalism. All this was true. And worse, that was not mentioned. Did they not read Italian, about bombs, about making them; he had written about this as well. Probably not. They did not detain him. He was freed with a fine only and with a warning. He must cease publishing his propaganda against the war. Harsher treatment was sure to come. There will be newer, harsher laws. Instead of a fine, would the next arrest lead to prison?

Had Erasmo not learned of this before? When there was war, there was fear. Fear that could be stoked by governments for their own ends. Ordinary people would willingly be suppressed. To feel safe from dangerous "elements" who might be among them, who might live next door, or in that section of town where ordinary law-abiding people did not venture. These fears could be useful to those in power, to put down those they labeled enemies of the state. This was an old story.

Another danger, my cousin, Cino said. There is a man at the Sanchinis' who left in a hurry after Luigi's arrest. He helped with printing the *Cronaca* and had to leave. He didn't know where to go, so Giobbe let him in.

This makes no sense, Cino. Why would he do that? You say we must be careful, but this is not careful. Erasmo was finding it difficult to remain calm.

We take care of our own. Giobbe would not turn him away. Anyway, Luigi is safe for the moment. I come to you today to issue a warning. Watch where you go, who you see. Do not come to me or go to the Sanchinis'. If necessary, I will get word to you.

Cino rose. At the door, he turned the sign to open. Tutto normale. Everything is to be normal. Calma, he said.

When Cino was gone, Erasmo raised the shade covering the window. Everything as normal. Except Erasmo's heart was still pounding.

* * *

Cino was good to his word. He stayed away from Erasmo. Erasmo stayed away from the Sanchinis. Lia was good, too. She stayed close to home, tending the babies and not complaining. She knew how to go underground, she told Erasmo. Which is what they all did. Several months went by in this way. Occasionally Cino got word to him. There was the man who came into the shop one day, closing the door quickly behind him, just as Erasmo was preparing to leave.

The man, small and compact, moved like a furtive animal. He said he needed a repair and gestured toward the back room.

In case someone comes in, he said, handing Erasmo his left shoe. He pointed to the leather top torn from the sole. They will see we have business.

Erasmo sat at his cobbler's bench and stitched while the man sat in the chair in the corner and talked.

He mentioned the young man who had fled to the Sanchinis' when Galleani was arrested. He said the man was named Carlo, and he had left again. No one seems to know where he is now, the man said. Good, Erasmo thought. And this man now in his shop, whose name was Silvio, was someone Erasmo did not know, but here he was, and he had come to say more.

In a town called Bay View in the place called Milwaukee, our comrades opposed, you could say, a church group who left their own neighborhood to cause trouble near our comrades' meeting place in their neighborhood. Our comrades, angry, took down, you could say 'tore down,' their American flag. The dirty priest who led them instigated trouble, an Italian, too. He called the police. Then there was fighting. Two of our men were shot dead there and then, by these police. But our people were the ones arrested and thrown in jail. And another one of ours was shot in the back, but he lives.

He looked for a place to spit. Erasmo slid a pot over with his foot. Erasmo listened intently, wondering where this place was and how he was coming to learn of it all the way on Cherry Street in New Britain, Connecticut. But there was more.

You know, shoemaker, that many of our comrades are in Mexico, Silvio went on. But, no, Erasmo did not know this. There had been so little contact with anyone, including Cino.

Yes, yes, Silvio said. Galleani is there and others. Men more experienced, you could say, in these things than we are. They are staying safe from America's authorities there, but they are very angry over the Milwaukee treatment of our comrades. There will be more to this story. Some say Carlo, the one who left the Sanchinis' home to go who-knows-where, is involved in a new plan, being hatched, there, in Mexico.

Silvio had come to the end of his news. Taking his newly repaired shoe from Erasmo, he said, There is no charge for your work, I think, since I came to be sure you are informed. Just remember, when you hear of other things happening, or soon to happen, you could say, these things are related. He laced up his shoe. And then he left.

Erasmo stood still for a moment, wondering why he had been informed. And he marveled at the way in which he had learned this news, all the way from a place called Milwaukee. And then he remembered the great man's words about many who shared their Beautiful Idea. Many, he said, who were spread across the country with the same purpose.

How much more of such news could they endure? Word came again to Erasmo that evening, after Silvio's visit, this time through Giù, who had been so far removed from any news it was hard to believe he was the one to tell Eramso and Lia about the Sanchinis—and Cino.

With Aldo and Nino asleep in their beds, the family of three adults was seated at the kitchen table, their dinner before them. Giù seemed nervous. He pushed the food on his plate. This was not unusual. He did this often because his appetite was not good. But then he told them he had decided to walk to Cino's earlier. It was a beautiful day and he felt better than he had in many weeks. He thought it would be a good idea to see his cousin.

But it was not a good idea, Giù said. Cino asked if I did not know we were staying apart. I told him, yes, I knew, but this was just a meeting of cousins on a beautiful day, nothing dangerous in that, no? And he told me, yes, dangerous. He spoke to me through the door, barely opened. He wouldn't let me in and said I should go home immediately and tell your brother, he said, and Lia, too that the Sanchinis have been arrested. They were gone. Their apartment empty. The police came and said they could not raise money for Galleani and his propaganda. They were un-American, the police told them. 'It's a free country,' Cino said to me, over and over. 'You can raise money for who you like. This is something else.'

He was very agitated, Giù said, looking down at the food still untouched on his plate.

Lia slammed her hand on the table and hissed through her teeth, turning her head away from the brothers.

Who is with the children? she asked, turning back to face Giù.

No, no, don't worry, Lia, he said. They are safe. They are with friends, in Boston, I think. That is what Cino said.

Erasmo remained silent. The Sanchinis were not arrested by the police, he reasoned. They were in Boston, arrested by federal agents.

What is happening? Where is everyone going? I don't understand any of this. Amalia rose from the table and began pacing in the small kitchen.

Why now? Why is everything suddenly so changed? She stopped to look at Giù. Did you ask about Giobbe and Irma? When will they be back?

Cino didn't say, Giù answered. He doesn't know, I think. No one knows. Cino finally opened the door just enough to let me in. I saw that Felice was not home—and the children, they were not there either. He had sent them to her mother's in Brooklyn, he told me. We went into the main room, and we sat in the dark. He had pulled the curtains closed. That's when he told me about his own troubles.

Erasmo and Lia listened as Giù continued. There was an Italian man who seemed friendly to Cino and the others who met at Cino's, in the back of his shop, where they always met. He wanted to join their cause, he said, but he was not what he seemed. A man called Silvio had found out that the man had been sent by federal agents who have been around asking questions. When he saw the man at Cino's, Silvio accused him of spying. Then there was a fight, but no one was hurt. Everyone just wanted to get out of there. And they did. But now Cino is waiting to be arrested, like the Sanchinis. He's afraid to leave his house.

Why doesn't he leave? Why is Cino waiting like a dog to be taken away? Lia asked.

Giù looked confused. I don't know, he said.

Because he is not a dog, said Erasmo. He lives here, in his own home, with his family. He is a businessman who is known in town. He is not an unknown immigrant. Why would he run, they would want to know. It would look bad. But Erasmo was also confused. Why did the man, Silvio, who came to tell him about the Sanchinis, not tell him about Cino? He knew more than he was telling. Did Cino not want Erasmo to know? Why?

Erasmo sat back in his chair. His hands were cold, and he drew his arms over this chest, saying nothing. What he was thinking he did not want to share. There were secrets within secrets. With Galleani and his closest men in Mexico and Cino so worried, their little game of cat and mouse had suddenly turned far more serious. They were being hunted by forces stronger, more powerful, and more cunning than their mouse. These were men who would stop at nothing. Erasmo had seen such men before at home in Italy, in much smaller ways, it was true, but when men know they have power, they are not afraid to use it. He did not share his thoughts with his wife or brother, but he knew his part in the game was not done. He knew this because Silvio had come to see him and had not told him about Cino. The hunted men were afraid, and fear did things to people. Mantieni la calma, é tutto normale, Cino had told him. But it was more difficult now, to be calm, to appear normal.

Eat, brother. Your food is getting cold. You, too, Lia. There's nothing we can do now. Be patient. Calma, Erasmo said, looking at Lia.

They continued this way, leading quiet lives. Cino was not arrested. He continued to work at his shop, but there were no more meetings. The Sanchinis returned in November, released with nothing more than a warning. The gruppo continued to meet at different places, careful not to call attention to themselves. It was all readings and speeches and singing sotto voce. Cino had long since apologized for not telling Erasmo about the spy in his shop.

'I wasn't going to tell Giù, but there he was standing at my door. What was I to do? I let him in, of course, and I told him.' This is what Cino told his cousin.

That was supposed to be the end of it, but Erasmo knew

better. He surmised that Cino wanted to keep fear from eating his cousin as it had been eating him. And why? Because there was more to come. Was this the calm before the storm? Erasmo was sure the storm was churning and gaining force. Normale? Calma? Nothing was what it seemed, certainly not normal, certainly not calm. And certainly they were still being watched.

Silvio came to Erasmo again, coming into the shop brushing snow from his coat. He too turned the sign to closed, as Cino had done months earlier. He too lowered the shade.

Silvio apparently was not worried about meetings between two Italian men, as most were these days, but nevertheless, he arrived taking precautions and knowing he would be leaving in the safety of darkness.

Do you need a repair? Erasmo asked.

Not this time. But I do have news from Cino. Bad news, you could say. No turning back now, shoemaker. Cino needs you.

✳ ✳ ✳

With all that he had heard, Erasmo climbed the stairs to his home, each step slow and deliberate. Would he tell Lia and how much? She remembered to be calm most days, but she simmered, like the sauce on the stove, and he didn't know how she would take this news. He had seen the sauce boil over before and was not eager to see it again.

In the end, when he told her what would be asked of him, with Giù and the babies asleep, there had been no scene. She simply said, no, you cannot.

Silvio's story had been, once again, about Milwaukee.

That man Carlo has been busy with the poof. This time his little bomb has started a war, you could say, he told Erasmo.

Those arrested in Bay View had been blamed for a bomb

that went off in the police headquarters in Milwaukee. This was no small bomb. Ten detectives and one woman were killed. They were all convicted, eleven for eleven, ten men and one woman. No matter that the bomb was never meant for the police, Silvio had told Erasmo. It was for that rat, the priest at the church. He was the one who caused all the trouble to begin with. The fate of the Bay View comrades was sealed. It didn't matter if the case against them was suspect. Even the papers reported on the symbolism of eleven for eleven. But the scene at the police station had been horrific.

When Erasmo asked how the bomb got to the police station. Silvio replied, Who knows? They said a little kid was told to carry it from the church to the police station. You can read it in the papers. People were standing on line to see a show when they heard the blast. One man who was holding his ears from the force heard shrieks from the jail. Some people on the street rushed over to help and began climbing through the mess in the dark. They didn't know the danger they were in. The whole thing could've crashed down on them. They lit matches so they could see, and kept going. They found some survivors but also bodies blown to bits. Who would tell a kid to do that? Does that make sense to you? Those pigs who sentenced our comrades cared nothing for the truth. Our people were convicted to send a message. The woman of ours was sentenced like the others. Her daughter was taken from her. Her family wanted the girl, but the state took her anyway. They want us to know they are on to us and our plans. These eleven of ours will pay for what happened at the police station.

Erasmo could barely get the words out to tell Lia all that he had heard. Lia, too, was shaken.

Dio mio, she cried, putting one hand over her chest, the other on the table to steady herself as she sat down. Erasmo and Lia sat with their hands folded on the table in front of them, each in thought, neither knowing what to make of it. But Erasmo knew one thing, something he had not mentioned until now.

This is the beginning, Erasmo said, not the end. Silvio said our group must get the dynamite and transport it to Carlo. We must be very careful. There are federal agents everywhere.

Why us? Doesn't he know we are remaining silent here?

And we've done it well. Cino was not arrested. The Sanchinis are back. But none of that matters. The order comes from Luigi. It must be done.

Amalia was silent. She looked away and began to moisten her lips. She was thinking, and she was seeing. Erasmo understood this.

What do you have to do with it, Ermo? she asked. And do not tell me pretty lies.

Erasmo drew a breath and told her. Cino wants me to get the dynamite. Many sticks of it, three dozen. Erasmo watched her. This is where the simmer will boil, he thought, but she only said no, you cannot.

And then she asked, Why not him? Why not Cino? He knows how these things work.

Erasmo took her hand and brought it to his lips.

Lia. You know. You know Cino can't do it, not after what happened in his shop. No one suspects me. No one, not after the fires, the papers, no one, not even now.

He realized he had never told her of the fires until now, but she didn't flinch. It was as if she had known it all along.

She was calm now, drawing her hand away. And where will you get dynamite and not be caught?

A little here, a little there. It will be arranged. I will follow instructions to the places I must go and wait to learn the rest. Cino will tell Silvio who will tell me.

I don't care. He should still do it himself. She pushed away from the table and began pacing back and forth in their little kitchen. The simmering was beginning to boil again. You are the one with babies who need their father, she said. You are the one caring for a sick brother. And me, Ermo, you have me. What would happen to me, to us, if you are caught? This is not just a fine. They could throw you in prison. Does Cino not think of these things?

Come, sit down, he said. It's me, Lia. I have to do it. Calma, please. Cino has a family. I'm not the only one.

No, Ermo. You cannot do it, she said again. And then she did what he had not seen her do before, not even when her father died. She covered her face with her hands. Her shoulders began to shake. His Lia, the bravest among them, cried.

Erasmo held her in his arms. There had been an incident in Milwaukee. What does a bomb in Milwaukee have to do with a shoemaker in New Britain, he wondered. He would do what he had been asked to do. And yet, he asked, why must it be me? He knew the risks. Dynamite. This was not tossing leaflets all over town, or setting fires in vacant buildings. This was pericoloso, perilous business. But of course, these doubts he kept to himself. There was more he would keep to himself.

* * *

This dreadful year came to an end at a warehouse outside of town. Erasmo was not eager to attend. He had done what he had been asked to do. The sticks of dynamite had been delivered to Carlo who was responsible for the remaining journey of this dangerous cargo. Erasmo wanted nothing more to do with it. His hands hadn't stopped shaking since the door of the Sanchinis' apartment was closed behind him.

It was a night of terrible snow, high winds, and bitter cold. Everyone thought Schiavina would never make it. After much singing and drinking, he did arrive, not long before the midnight celebration. They gathered around to hear him tell the assembled guests what they must be prepared to endure. Their war was underway, and they must endure it together. No one is safe unless all of us are true to the Idea. All across the country, each is a part of one strong, indomitable force. It is now, my comrades. The Beautiful Idea is in reach.

He finished in time for the ringing of the bells, which could be heard from the center of the town. Inside, among those gathered, the celebration was muted. Buon anno, they said to each other, felice anno nuovo. They drank wine from their glasses and became quiet as the ringing of the bells faded away.

It was strange, Erasmo thought. Whenever Lia talked about that night, all she remembered was the singing.

7

UN SOGNO INFRANTO

New Britain, Connecticut
June 29, 1995

I'm going to tell you something now about the beginning of
our end. We thought after the arrests and the eyes on our
cousin and friends that things would be calm. We hoped our
war would continue but underground, no more attention to us
in our little town. It was a foolish dream, one that in 1918
would break, taking with it our hearts, our broken hearts.

But first I must tell you how I knew terrible things were
coming, a premonition of the malocchio that would torment us.

I should have known when Ermo got so sick, a nfruenza, a
terrible case, the flu, influenza, worse than I had ever seen. He
came upstairs from work one bitter cold night early in January,
and he collapsed when he came inside. Giù and I were able to
get him up and into bed. I took off his clothes, he was burning. I
washed him and got him into a nightshirt, but the fever roared.
He couldn't eat or drink. I had to cut ice chips to put on his
parched lips and try to get as much of it into his mouth as I

could. He coughed and made terrible noises in his throat, like he was drowning.

Giù was taking care of the babies while I tended to Ermo, but I was worried about him, too. What if he got this terrible fever and cough? I knew he would die, so I kept him away. I stayed behind our bedroom door with Ermo, who was getting worse. Just touching his skin burned my hand. I kept putting cold cloths on his head and body and keeping him covered with the blanket because in spite of the raging fever, he shivered until his teeth rattled.

In this fevered way, his mind was full of dreams. He mumbled things I couldn't understand. He tossed his head from side to side, arched his back, fell back on his pillow, and was silent for a time. But then his dreams took him home to his mother. He called her by name, Nicoletta, he said over again. He spoke of the famous painter from long ago, the one on his mother's side. He painted for the church and for the rich. I heard Ermo say in his dream that he saw Christ. The famous painter died in the plague many years ago, centuries ago. I wondered if Ermo dreamed of him because he was so sick. Ermo was still again, but then he called for his mamma. And this scared me because it happens when a man is dying, he calls for his mother.

After some days of this, I had to send Giù to the store for a remedy, more than the ice I chipped from the icebox, more than the cold wash rags to lower his fever. He had had nothing to eat but a few spoonsful of soup a day, and even that was hard to get into him. In those days, you didn't call the doctor unless you were having a baby or dying, and maybe not even then. What if they sent you to the hospital? Then it was certain you would die.

Ermo was very bad, and even though it was so cold, I had to

send Giù, who was never well. But he had to go. I worried. Maybe soon I would be taking care of two.

When he came back, I took the packages from him and sent him to care for the boys. By now their beds were in a room Ermo had made for them by walling in a space from our sitting room. It was nice, with a little bed for Aldo and Nino's crib. There was even a little dresser for their clothes. We were a growing family, but we could take care of ourselves. We always had enough to eat and clothes on our backs. We had these things that others did not, and we were, we were once, happy. Even with the injustice and unfairness that we fought, we were happy. But now everything was changing.

In the kitchen, I took the basil, a lot of it, and ginger and some honey and boiled them into a drink that I would have to find a way to make him swallow. It was a very strong brew, the smell like basil, but boiled down so very pungent. And with the ginger, only the honey made it a little sweet. I waited for it to cool just enough for him to drink. In the bedroom, I propped up his pillow and tried to hold him with my arm behind his back, my hand cradling his neck. With my free hand, I put the cup to his lips. He tried, but he was so weak, it was hard for him to swallow. He went into a coughing fit. I propped his pillow up more and waited. With one hand I pried open his mouth and with the other I gently poured in some of the drink. I hoped he would not cough again. I gave him just enough so that he could swallow one little sip at a time, until finally he took it all.

Back then to the kitchen. Next, I crushed the garlic and crushed and crushed, adding olive oil, just enough until I made a paste, l'unguento. The smell was so strong, I cried, garlic tears mixing with my own. I made the paste thick enough to spread all over Ermo's chest. He was too weak to say no to me. I did what I had to do. I even rubbed it into his feet, the way Mamma did when I was little.

The last treatment was the steam. I made a boiling pot of timo, the herb, thyme. It made the kitchen smell of medicine, but good, a clean smell. Again, in the bedroom, I propped him up on his pillow and covered him under a blanket with that boiling pot of timo near his chest on the bed. It was a balancing act, I tell you. At any moment he might move, or have a wracking cough, and it would spill the hot liquid everywhere, but it was good. Right away, I heard his breathing getting better.

I did this round the clock for three more days, the drink, the paste, the steam. The kitchen smelled like a restaurant one minute, a hospital the next, but by the fourth morning, Ermo was no longer out of his head. The fever broke. We were so happy the first night he got up and ate his dinner with us. And then he would get stronger everyday.

I did not get sick. Not the babies, and thankfully, neither did Giù.

But I did not forget this illness that was an omen. Soon the big flu would come, but this was our nfruenza, the one that foretold our future.

Before long Ermo was back at work. We stayed in our own neighborhood, but even there, resentment was growing. Many of Ermo's customers stopped coming. Some of our Italian neighbors were for the rising leader in Italy, Mussolini. To us he was already a fascist, and our gruppo despised him. Cino wrote letters against him in Galleani's *Cronaca*. We spit when his name was mentioned. There were others in our neighborhood who wanted to kiss the feet of the Americans and who joined the war, who signed up, who gave in to pressure, and there was a lot. I tell you now how we felt then. Of course as time went on, we would try to forget those days, the days when we had ideals and dreams for a better world.

January of 1918 was a very bad month. Did I tell you? I

forget sometimes how much I have already said. This is the month that Ella was arrested. I was beside myself when I heard the news. I was in the market to buy a bone to make soup for Ermo, who was still not fully himself, and people were talking about a woman, an anarchist in Chicago, who had been arrested with thirty-six sticks of dynamite. The papers always wrote about enemy aliens and bombs to work people up. That's what sold papers. I stopped to listen but didn't want to sound too interested. It could be dangerous to call attention to myself.

Something told me it was Ella. I became very worried about my friend. And she was my friend. She would come over sometimes. We would sit on the stoop of our building outside Erasmo's shop. He didn't like it, but we did it anyway. I told him no one suspected us of anything. We were just two young women enjoying some time out of the house. We talked about everything. She asked me what it was like to have babies. She said she wanted to be a mother one day. She said Augusto didn't want children, but maybe she would have a baby anyway. I didn't know what she meant, but she was like that, a free thinker. And so was I. I just laughed when she said it. When the weather was cold, she stopped coming. And I missed her.

Now People at the market were talking about this young woman in Chicago. There was a newsboy outside. I gave him two pennies and took a paper. In big letters, there it was, "Dynamite Girl Arrested in Chicago." Dynamite Girl. That's what they called her. But they didn't know who she was or where she was from, not at first. Such a good actress. She told them she was Linda Jose. That was the name of one of the characters in one of our plays. When I read that I knew for sure it was Ella.

Thirty-six sticks of dynamite were found in her valise in Chicago. Why was she in Chicago with those sticks? I tell you the truth, that Ermo never told me about any plan for the dynamite. Maybe he never knew, either. All I know is Augusto, who was her husband and Cino's friend, disappeared. We never heard from him again. And Ella became famous. She was in newspapers all over the country. They made her sound like a gangster's girl, but she was no gangster. Even then, if you were Italian, you were a gangster, before the Mafia in the movies. People didn't know who we were or what we believed, what we were fighting for. But one thing is sure, we weren't gangsters.

She told them she didn't believe in God or government or wars. They said she was an anarchist through and through. But did they know what that meant? What's the use? They didn't know then, and they don't know now. We were dreamers. We dreamed of a better world, after the priests and politicians and all those who poison and imprison our brains were gone. But Ella. I think people liked reading about her, even if they had to say she was an enemy alien. Eventually the police figured out who she was and where she was from. Did she ever tell them about us? I don't know, I don't think so, but it was a dangerous time for us then. We waited for what would happen next. She was there in Chicago for months, until her trial. Ella, young, beautiful Ella. People used to say we could've been sisters. We were so much alike. We were pretty and loved books and learning. She was married young, like me. It could've been me, going to Chicago with thirty-six sticks of dynamite, but I wasn't chosen. I had babies.

The cops questioned and questioned her. Then she had a trial and then she went to jail. Oh how I cried. But to tell you the truth, I cried my heart out then over so much more. Things that happened to her on certain dates happened to Ermo and Giù, too, on those dates. I haven't forgotten them. Important dates, June and October, 1918. I'll tell you more. Later. But what about us, all of us, after they found out who she was? Oh

Maronn, what happened. All those months Ella was in jail, the feds were all over us.

We went deeper underground. Cino wouldn't see us. He sent Silvio to tell Ermo that Cino wanted him to do a deed, to place dynamite in a newspaper office downtown. Ermo wanted to know who told Cino it had to be done. Silvio said, non chiedere niente, meaning Ermo wasn't supposed to ask, but he did, and when he found out the order didn't come from the great man, Ermo said no. Cino was not his boss, so he said no. I was glad, too, that Ermo said no.

That was in the spring, after our gruppo wrote a letter for Luigi's *Cronaca*, one of the last. In it, we said that we would wait for 'better weather.' Everyone knew what that meant. In New Britain we had to stay low, and we did. But then in May, it was terrible. Giobbe and Irma and Cino were arrested. They had all been under surveillance as anarchists since the Sanchinis other arrest. They were taken to Boston again by the feds, Cino, too, this time. We were finished. In New Britain we were finished, but New Britain wasn't finished with us. They were all released but it wasn't over. In time the Sanchinis and Luigi, our great man, would eventually be deported, never Cino, though. He was free.

But not us. We would never be free again.

8

IL LAMENTO

New Britain
January 1918

C risto, Cristo, he called out. He did not believe in God or the Son of God or of any son of any god of any religion. But he knew he was calling the name, the word, but not the Word or the Son. The image is not the thing. Made in God's image is not God. An image of Christ is not Christ.

Where was he now? He remembered walking, each step a journey of many miles, a great mountain to climb. He remembered walking into his home, his refuge. Was that Lia, who cried out when he fell, who picked him up? Not Lia. She was too small. It must have been Giù. But who was with him now, by his bed? He was home. It was his mother. He could smell the herbs from her garden, pungent and sweet, both those things. Like home, pungent and sweet. He longed for it now. Would the image who was not the Son help him, the son, be in the arms of his mother, not the mother who comforted her Son in the image? Compianto sul Cristo morto. Lamentarsi. His own mother did *not lament. She only spoke of the artist of the image of the Son and the mother. Hundreds of years ago but every uncle and aunt, every cousin since spoke of him, the one who was from there, who bore the family name, who painted the Son and the mother.*

He knew it made his mother proud that she was not a commoner. She ran her bar with great authority. Everyone in their town knew her and respected her. My uncle painted Cristo, she would say, as if he were her father's brother. And the Virgin and many saints, she said. He painted them for the church. This great painter was from a town only thirty kilometers away from our hometown. He was a knight, a cavaliere. You are descended from a great man, she told her sons. But Erasmo cared not for such talk. His mother, like most women, not Ella or Lia, but most, went on and on about God and saints. But certainly not Erasmo, himself named after a saint whose church was in their neighborhood. If he did not believe in the son of god then he did not believe that any man was above him, even a knight or a painter of the man who was cristo.

He was parched, hot, then cold. Then the smell of his mother's garden. His mother. Nicoletta. Mamma. He called to her. He saw her in her garden, gathering herbs and tomatoes and oranges. He smelled them and that is how he knew he was home. He began to breathe more easily.

The first night Erasmo was well was on a Sunday. He joined Lia, who was not eating but holding Nino who was crying, and Giù who was already eating his dinner of pasta and beef, a rare treat.

I made braciole, said Lia, rocking Nino, who had stopped crying. She didn't comment on Erasmo's illness or that he was out of bed and coming to eat. But she looked up at him and her smile said what she did not.

I will set a place for you. She rose to take Nino to his crib, but Erasmo stopped her.

Let me take him. It's all right. I am well now. She gave his son to him.

There's not much meat, but enough for us tonight, she said on her way to the kitchen. You must eat the biggest share, to get your strength back.

Erasmo wondered why there was not enough meat but said nothing. Many thoughts were confusing him. He must come to each one at a time. When the three were seated, he asked what day it was. He didn't know how long he had been sick.

* * *

Amalia and Giuseppe looked at each other. So much had happened in the days of Erasmo's illness. It would be hard to tell him.

You have been in bed for eight days, Ermo, said Amalia.

But what about the shop? Who was taking care of the customers? He said this knowing his business had fallen since the war and its hysteria, and the draft had turned neighbor against neighbor. Italian boys signing up to fight a stupid war with no just cause to prove they were American patriots. Erasmo could hardly contain his disdain.

It's all right, brother, said Giuseppe. I have been in the shop every day. He paused to choose his words. It has been not so good, with customers, but there have been some—some who are not like the others. And I think we will make enough to get by. This war won't last forever.

Has there been enough to eat? Erasmo asked, worried that during his illness his family had gone hungry.

Nothing like that, Ermo. We have enough.

Erasmo leaned over to place a hand on his brother's shoulder. Thank you, Giù, he said. I hope you have been well. The air in the shop is bad sometimes, too closed up, and the polish and dust could make you cough.

It is okay. My cough is not so bad. Maybe I am better, he said.

Giuseppe smiled, a little, and looked to Amalia who shook her head so slightly, surely she thought Erasmo did not see it. But Giuseppe saw her and nodded back.

Whatever else they had to say would wait. Erasmo knew there was more to come, but he wasn't ready to ask. His body was weak and sore, as it was after a bad fight with a strong opponent, but that he could take. What he couldn't take was the confusion in his brain. What he knew was not enough to answer all his questions.

Lia never knew the details about his journey to get the dynamite, only that he was gone for three days. She knew he would not tell her. She knew he was protecting her and the babies, but something in her had changed. She felt betrayed, he knew, not because there were things she could not know, but because from the beginning of the plan, she had been cut out of the very deeds that would bring to life the Beautiful Idea, the one that included not only men, but women, the dream that meant total freedom, no more prisons of the body or the mind. From the beginning, the Sanchinis, the gruppo, Ella, and Luigi —the words and the man—they had formed her. Everything she believed and stood for, all of it, came from them and their commitment to the Idea.

Erasmo thought of this betrayal, and it cut into him. But even he, involved in the deed, did not know the details—and this cut deeper. Silvio had brought him a slip of paper with addresses, dates and times, no names. These five places were arranged as a list, one date and place per line. When you leave one place, tear it off the list and make it into little pieces to throw away, Silvio told him. When Erasmo questioned him, Silvio only said it is better not to know too much.

Erasmo was to arrive at each of these places precisely at the time noted. It had all been carefully arranged, Silvio told him. He was to take the package handed to him, put it into his bag, and move to the next location on the slip of paper. He did this by train and by cars that were there to drive him to each new location, twice staying the night in the home of someone he did not know, and then in the morning going to the next train station, until he arrived in Youngstown where he was met by Carlo who took his grip, the canvas bag with two leather handles, the one Erasmo had carried on the ship from Naples, this grip now containing the thirty-six sticks of dynamite. There he spent the last night. He stayed up late talking to Carlo about these terrible times, about Milwaukee, about the danger Luigi faced, all of them. He told Erasmo why he was chosen to follow a maze, to confuse the cat, he said.

And you were the strongest to do this work. Your other jobs were done well. And you are the least known among us.

This Erasmo thought may have been the true strength he brought. Now we will lie low, Carlo told him, until the next step in the plan. Until you get home, and we know no one has followed you. You will take the train directly home in the morning, he told Erasmo.

But Carlo told him no more. Not the next step, perhaps the one to get the cat.

Erasmo went home with his grip empty of its heavy cargo, filled now with old newspapers mimicking the heft of contents. Just in case he had been seen, he would arrive as he had left, a traveling man. Opening the door to their apartment, he gave Lia the empty grip a week before his illness struck.

It took several days after the braciole before Amalia said Erasmo was strong enough to know about the ever-growing danger that was surely awaiting the New Britain followers of Luigi Galleani.

Silvio had kept them informed during Erasmo's illness. He was a sly, slight man who moved in shadows and light, pressing himself against walls until he seemed to disappear. He was one of them, but he did not participate in the gruppo. No one seemed to know him. Rather, he was known to be a friend of Cino's, one Cino had cultivated for this very reason, to carry and to receive messages. He was Italian, but he was not on any lists. The important thing was that he never get caught. In that way his loyalty would never be tested.

When Erasmo was well enough, Silvio came again with more details, more than Amalia or Giù knew. Here in his shop is what Erasmo was to learn from Silvio:

You procured, you might say, the sticks, and that was good. You did your part to punish the criminals in Milwaukee for what they did to us. Now it would be up to Ella to take it further yet. Who would suspect such an innocent-looking, thin stripe of a girl? She and Augusto left here for Youngstown, where she would pick up your bambini, one could say, right where you left them. They waited there patiently until the next caretaker. Ella was going to take your babies to the next destination. Very careful, you see, no one the wiser. They have their eyes everywhere, and we have ours. We know them, how they work. They still do not know our ways, but they are learning. So, there in Youngstown, Ella and Augusto met Carlo and Mario, you don't know him, but he is very important to the cause. They stayed a day or two, but when it was time to go, Mario gave the sticks, your babies to Ella. Augusto left. We don't know where he is, but you will see, because of events, he must not be found.

At the station, Ella and Carlo and the black valise left for another destination to make sure no one was watching. They went to a town for one night. It was part of the plan that they would stay at a hotel as husband and wife. Here I will tell you, Carlo and Ella, they fucked, hanno scopato. It was a problem, which you will see. But he left her at the station the next afternoon. So little Ella and the black valise left alone for Chicago. Now the trouble starts. And this is why things now are so bad. Ella was arrested in Chicago.

Erasmo could not believe what he was hearing. His first reaction was to look to the door leading up his apartment. He didn't want Lia to know. But of course she knew. This is what she and Giù were keeping from him.

Silvio continued while Erasmo could barely hear because of the blood pounding in his ears. With Ella in jail, they were all in danger. She knew it all. What would they do to her to make her talk?

Somehow she caused suspicion, Silvio said. The porter tricked her out of the compartment on the train where she was staying alone. He went in and opened the black valise under her seat. He saw your sticks there and called the police.

Now Erasmo was not happy to hear the dynamite referred to as his. He asked Silvio how this could have happened. How did a porter know to trick her and to look in the valise? Did someone tip the porter off? After all the trips to make sure no one was watching, a porter on the train, grew suspicious and turned her in?

Silvio shook his head. You are right, shoemaker. It doesn't add up. There's a snake somewhere.

Oddio, said Erasmo, not used to calling on God. What happens now?

You must keep working, stay to your normal routine. Normale, remember? Same as before. We will get word to you when necessary. Don't contact anyone. Don't contact Cino. Not you, not Giuseppe. Capisci, shoemaker?

This tone sounded like a threat that Erasmo didn't like, but he let it go. Let the slippery little man leave now. He would need his information later.

One more thing Silvio was to add before going. We are all in her hands now. And you should know, forget Augusto. She loves Carlo. Love complicates things. Our fate is in the hands of a skinny little girl in love.

Erasmo nodded. He didn't ask how Silvio knew what was in Ella's heart. He was thinking of the thirty-six sticks in the black valise.

9

IL LAMENTO, DUE

New Britain
June 1918

By June, everything Erasmo knew of his life in America would be taken from him. He began to curse the dream of a better life, not the one that came with the promise of America, but the other dream, the one he learned to love after he fell in love with Amalia, the beautiful girl who was a woman at the Sanchinis'. That dream, the Idea, he had fallen in love with when he fell in love with her, and that dream had brought him here, to this time of trouble.

He had learned too late to say no to Cino. In early May, when Silvio had come to him again and told him he was to plant a poof, this one in the newspaper office downtown, Erasmo had said no. Maybe from that day on his fate was sealed. He didn't know. All he knew was Cino was hiding out in plain sight and giving his own orders. Erasmo had held firm. He would follow the great man, not Cino. But it was earlier, in January, when he had done the great man's bidding that things had begun to fall apart, when Ella was arrested, when their fate was in her hands. These were not the days of the gruppo, when they sang, went to lectures, and put on plays. This year there had been no May Day festa. There was no Beautiful Idea now.

Someone planted the poof in the newspaper office, but it wasn't Erasmo. No one was hurt, and the police didn't seem to know who did it. Worse news came when he learned the Sanchinis had been arrested again. A new law said it was a crime to speak against the war. No words, not speech, not newspapers, or pamphlets like Luigi's could speak the truth now about an insane war profiting on common men, on boys barely old enough to shave. A man, or woman, could be put in jail or deported for saying it. This would no doubt be the fate of Giobbe and Irma.

It was not the Sanchinis alone who were arrested and brought to Boston for questioning. It was Cino, too. He was there when the feds came, banging on the door, finding all the antiwar and anti-draft materials. It was in the newspapers. It was Silvio who came with the news and told Erasmo that Cino had long been under suspicion. Neighbors said he did no work and yet had a big Buick machine. What did they think, that anarchists were rich and didn't work? It was ridiculous, of course Cino worked. Erasmo waved off any suspicions about Cino, but he did wonder why his own business was suffering while Cino's was doing well. Money was not an issue for Cino as it was for Erasmo. He bristled when he thought of Lia counting her pennies at the market.

Look, shoemaker, Silvio had told him then, it's over now. Forget the gruppo. Cobble, you and your brother, and stay out of it from now on. Silvio left as he came, in shadows, but more comprensivo in his manner, Erasmo thought. What had got into him, this near stranger who could at times be almost rude to a man in his own home, now almost understanding?

Silvio said they were to go about their business and work. That is what he and Giù had been doing since Erasmo had a nfruenza. Work, what little there was to do, they did, and stay low, normale, that is what they tried to do. But what was normale now?

Oh to have those earlier days again. To work, to climb the stairs, with whatever worry, doubts, and fears they had. It was a dream of its own, those days. With Lia waiting, sauce on the stove, the bambini waiting to see Papà. All gone, all gone.

On June 3, 1918, police came knocking. This scene would remain with Erasmo. He would from that day on hear Lia's words tumbling from her lips. Che succede? She would ask over again, not knowing what was happening.

He didn't either, but her voice trembling, fear he could not stop, that haunts him now, thinking back on it.

Silenzio, he whispers to her the first time she asks. Calma.

He tiptoes downstairs to open the door just a crack. He sees two policemen, one he knows. A beat cop, Officer Dolan. What do you want? Erasmo asks them.

The other one, the one he hasn't seen before, says, Did you know a man has been shot and stabbed and is now lying outside, nearly dead, in the yard next door?

No ... I don't know this ... I sleep in my house, with my wife, Erasmo says. He thinks but does not say, there were always drunken parties next door. The ones put on by that ridiculous woman, Cora Necchi, the one who enraged Erasmo when Lia was pregnant with Nino. He wonders if the man in her yard is nearly dead or merely drunk.

There's been some commotion here, not one a man could easily sleep through, this policeman says.

Just then a police wagon pulls up, and this other policeman takes this opportunity to push through the open door and to rush up the stairs. Erasmo sees Amalia at the top. She lets out a little scream and starts toward the bedroom where the babies are. Erasmo wants to go after her behind the policeman, but now Officer Dolan stops him and asks, Is Joseph here?

Not comfortable with conversations in English, Erasmo is confused and asks, Who is here?

Your brother, Joseph, Giussepe—is he here? The officer with me is going for Joseph.

Sì, yes, he is upstairs, sleeping.

Erasmo races up the stairs to see about his brother, about Amalia and the children. His home is under siege. The policeman Erasmo doesn't know is now in his house and says to him, Look, you better get your brother and get dressed. You may be in some trouble here, so do what I say.

Amalia comes into the small sitting room, closing the children's door behind her. Erasmo can see she is near panic. If it were not for the children, she would be screaming at these men in her house, but now for the babies, she is afraid. What is happening, Ermo? she pleads. Che succede?

In a soft voice, not to alarm her further, Erasmo stays with the policeman and says to his wife, Vai, Lia, vai. Go, wake Giù. He must get dressed.

Amalia nods and does as he asks.

By now Aldo and Nino are awakened and begin to cry. Erasmo cannot bear this happening in his own home. He goes to their door, but the policeman Erasmo does not want in his house steps in front of him.

Not so fast, he tells him.

Erasmo turns back to the closed door. This man will not tell him what to do in his own home. The policeman yields and tells him to say his goodbyes but to leave the door open. Goodbyes, Erasmo knows what that means. He is leaving his home with these policemen. He is being arrested, as the others have been. But he feels certain he will be back. The others were arrested, but they were released. It will be okay, he tells himself.

Erasmo goes first to Aldo who is sitting up in his little bed. Erasmo holds him and tells him everything is okay, that he must not be sad.

Mamma will always be here to take good care of you, he says.

He picks up Nino to comfort him and soon his crying stops. Erasmo smiles at them. They are calm. Erasmo leaves the room and quietly closes the door behind him.

I will go to my brother now, he tells the policeman, who nods.

Giù is up, confused, but he is dressing. Erasmo tells him what is happening. He tells him not to worry. Cino will take care of everything.

Amalia knocks on Giù's door and goes in. That policeman is searching everywhere, she tells them. Dolan is here, but the other one is downstairs searching. What is he looking for?

Erasmo doesn't know, he tells her. Maybe for books and literature, the way they did when they searched Giobbe's house, looking for Luigi's *Cronaca,* remember?

Yes, she says.

The policeman Erasmo doesn't know is back now and knocks loudly on Giù's door. Come out from there. That's enough talking. It's time to go, he says.

Aldo and Nino begin to cry again.

Erasmo looks toward their door. Go where? he asks.

The injured man is being taken to the hospital. You and your brother will follow. The man, the one shot and stabbed, he will be questioned, and you both will be present. Say goodbye to your wife.

The sound of the children crying becomes louder. Amalia rushes over to Erasmo and clings to him. The first policeman pushes her away. Erasmo raises his hand to him but Amalia stops him.

That would be a very bad idea, the policeman says. He grabs Erasmo forcefully and begins pushing him down the stairs. Giù, not putting up a fight, follows. At the door, Dolan stops and pulls Erasmo back a few steps and talks to him quietly. He offers assurances.

I was on the beat tonight, he says. Don't worry. I know you were home all night.

The other policeman, who didn't hear what Dolan said, tells him to watch out. That man is under arrest. He isn't your buddy, he says.

Erasmo is angry but stays silent. This is America, the land of the free? Of free speech? He is enraged as they leave, an anarchist's rage. But he is also worried now. An injured man. Will Erasmo and Giù be accused of hurting him? This is not the same thing as having anarchist literature in your home. This has nothing to do with being an anarchist. Why would anyone think he and Giù would shoot and stab a man?

As Erasmo is pushed into the back of the police wagon, he looks toward the apartment and sees the light on in the boys' room. He can still see the small tear on Aldo's cheek and smell the milk in the crease of Nino's neck. And Lia. There was a new baby growing inside her.

10

THIS TEEMING SHORE

New Britain
July 13, 1995

Y ou know, even now, telling you what comes next, my
arms grow limp. I sometimes, even now, cannot breathe
when I think of it, that night in June. A terrible knocking on our
door. Enough to wake the dead. We were all asleep. They
would never believe it, but it was true. We heard nothing that
was going on next door. We didn't know, and we didn't care.
We weren't friends with that terrible woman who was our
neighbor, Cora Necchi. She always had parties. They drank
and played cards to all hours. Erasmo hated her. But who knew
then that we would not be able to ignore her ever again?

You can read about it in the papers, the arrest. But I will tell
you, when they knocked on our door and forced their way into
our home, we did not know what was going on next door. The
one policeman I knew was Dolan, but the other one I didn't
know. Carlson was his name, I found out later. He told us a
man had been shot and stabbed and was lying in her yard. But

still we didn't know what that had to do with us. I was wondering if we had any of Luigi's papers with us. It was against the law to have his words on any paper. I wanted to find it and hide it. But there was no time. They searched and searched our house but found nothing, not that time. But they would come back, later, after Ermo and Giù were gone.

When the police took Ermo and Giù, I thought I would die. The babies were screaming and I was beside myself. I didn't know what the police knew about the fires or the other things Ermo had done. I hoped they would be released, like Cino and Giobbe and Irma, but how could I know? I searched the house for Luigi's pamphlets. I burned them in the sink. As soon as I got rid of the ashes, the police were back banging for me to open up. I screamed through the door, What do you want? I was afraid to open it. What if they took me? I knew that in Milwaukee, they took the mother away from her children. They kept banging, in the name of the law, they said.

I finally opened the door a crack, but they pushed through. It was Carlson and another one, but not Officer Dolan this time, someone else was with him. They began tearing through the house, every room, the shop, the basement. I was glad I had burned everything. There was nothing left to prove we were Galleanisti. They never mentioned the smell of fire still in the apartment. No, they were after something else. They took Giù's little knife from his room, a kitchen knife, and two of Ermo's guns, one that was broken and another small one. Carlson went down to the basement and left the other policeman upstairs with me. When he came back up, he had something else, something wrapped in a cloth that he said he found in a small space in the rocks. He held the bundle up and pointed downstairs. It was clear to me they were up to some-thing, but I didn't know what. I didn't know what it was in the wrapped cloth. And then they left. I waited up all night. Ermo and Giù didn't come home. It was the first night they did not come home. Every night that followed I waited and cried all night. I had a baby coming and that baby knew nothing but sorrow all those months she was in my belly and all those months after when she would be my youngest, my bambina.

* * *

The day after the arrest, Silvio came. Not Cino. I wanted Cino to come, but Silvio said not yet. He will see you soon, but not yet. I let Silvio come upstairs. He always stayed in the shop with Ermo, but I let him come up. I even made him coffee. We sat in the little sitting room. It was much smaller after Ermo made the bedroom for the babies. Silvio had come with a message, to tell me what was happening, that Ermo and Giù were not arrested for having Luigi's papers. They were arrested for murder.

I think I lost my mind then. I couldn't breathe, I was so confused, I could barely think. Who did they murder? Did Luigi tell them to kill someone? They didn't kill anyone, I screamed. Why would Luigi do this to them? But no, I wasn't thinking straight. Silvio told me it had nothing to do with Luigi. It was Cora's brother who had been killed. Frank, I screamed. Why would they kill Frank? Was Frank the man lying in Cora's yard, the man who had been shot and stabbed?

Then I thought of the policeman, and the things they took, the knives and the guns and the thing wrapped in the cloth.

Yes, Silvio said, it was Frank Palmese. He was dead and he accused Erasmo and Giuseppe at the hospital before he died.

I jumped up out of my chair and began pacing the floor. I held my hand over my mouth and closed the babies' door. It was pazzia. The whole idea was crazy. Erasmo would never kill Frank. And Giù was too sick to kill anyone.

This was the beginning of our end. Silvio tried to calm me, but I was out of my mind. No one could calm me. To be accused of being an anarchist was one thing but to be accused of murder, that was something very different. Murder was not an idea. I told Silvio I had to talk to Cino. He had to help us. Silvio made me sit down. He stroked my hair. I turned and pulled away so fast, I startled him. You, leave, I told him, and he slinked away. This is what will happen now, I thought. Ermo is not here to protect us.

I kept thinking Cino would come, but after a few days I couldn't take it anymore. I was afraid after the awful night of the police, when Frank was found bleeding in Cora's yard. After that night, some people came and rang the bell. I peeked through the curtain in the boys' room to see that it wasn't Cino and then backed away from the window. I knew we had neighbors, a few, Italian and some others, who were good, but I was afraid to go down to open the door, and to tell you the truth, I was ashamed. What if people believed it was true, that Ermo and Giù did those awful things to Frank? Through a tiny opening in the drawn curtain, every day I saw people going to Cora's house, bringing her food and flowers. Then I saw a big car pick her up for Frank's funeral. She screamed and shook her fist at our house. I backed away even though no one could see me. I was afraid someone might throw rocks or worse, start a fire maybe. But no one did any of those things.

I was desperate to talk to Cino, so I walked. I dressed the boys, and quickly left, hoping no one would see me. And we walked. Aldo walked and I carried Nino. Sometimes I carried both. It was hot, and I had to stop every few steps for Aldo to rest. A few motorcars passed us by, covering us in dust. One stopped and asked to give us a ride, but I said no. I didn't trust anyone. We got there. We must have looked terrible because when Felice opened the door she cried when she saw us.

She was very kind. She made me sit down and took the babies to give them something to drink. After they were playing on the floor, she brought me water. I didn't tell her about the new baby, but she could tell. I was sick, could hardly keep the water down. I told her, yes. A new baby was on the way. She held my hand, but I had come to see Cino, not to cry. I had been doing enough of that. She rose immediately and went to the shop to get him.

He, too, was kind and concerned for me and the babies. He apologized for not coming. I told him I didn't want Silvio coming anymore, but I didn't tell him why. He told me not to worry, that Ermo and Giù would soon be home. I wondered how he knew this. He seemed calmer than he had been. Not so worried anymore, but just the month before he had been arrested with the Sanchinis, and they had left. Where did they go, I asked? They left, and you are here. Why aren't you afraid?

We must not be afraid, he said. We are underground now, but things will change in our favor. Everyone will come back. The Sanchinis will come back. They're with relatives until things quiet down. You must believe that, he told me. You have been so brave, like our Ella. She is very brave.

That is when he told me that Ella would not be home soon. She was in Chicago still and had been charged with a serious crime. The same day that Ermo and Giù were taken away. That's the day she was charged with a crime, for having the dynamite. She will stay in jail there. We don't know when she will be back, he said. But she is good. She hasn't told them anything, and she won't, we know that. So we too, all of us, we must be brave.

I didn't see how Ella had anything to do with Ermo and Giù being accused of murdering poor Frank. I told Cino I was confused. And he said, of course, it is all a terrible mistake. And he promised to help me, to let me know what was happening.

He had a new telephone in his shop. No one had phones then, no one I knew. He said he would make calls and find out what he could. He would go to the jail in Hartford and see them. He said he would take me too as soon as he could.

And then I cried. I took his hand and kissed it. I was so grateful. He took me and the boys home in his Buick.

He was good to his word. No more Silvio. A week later, he came himself to tell me he was allowed to see them. I was feeding the boys when he came. I put them in their beds and came to sit by Cino so I could hear every word.

They are well, he began to tell me. He knew I would ask if they were eating. He was quiet and said yes, but they are not so hungry. I knew he would not tell me how bad it was. He said they had nothing to do but wait, to find out what would happen to them. Erasmo couldn't believe Frank was dead. He didn't think he would die. He said he tried to talk to Frank in Italian at the hospital, but the doctor stopped him. The doctor and the police spoke to Frank and to Ermo and to Giù only in English.

I thought of Ermo's English. He got by, but it was so hard for him to say in English what he wanted to say. But in Italian, he could say anything. He knew people thought he was stupid because his English wasn't good, but he was not. He was very smart. My heart was breaking, and Cino said he would take me to see them.

How hard those days were. Everything was falling apart. I had the apartment and the boys and the shop to worry me. I tried to run the shop myself, but I could only give customers back the shoes they had left to be repaired. There was a good neighbor, his name was Charles, I remember, and his wife, Jenny, yes. They were not Italian, but they were good people. They lived next to Cora, but they were not friends of hers. They came to the door many times, when I wasn't answering, but Charles, when he saw some people coming into the shop to pick up their shoes, he came too. And he offered to help there. He wasn't a cobbler, but he said he would polish and talk to customers and clean up. Maronn, what a help he was, and his wife, she came every day and brought food and sometimes a cake. I came to trust her. I didn't tell her everything about us, only about our troubles and how Ermo and Giù were innocent. She said not to worry. They were reading about the case in the newspapers, and there was reason to be hopeful. One reporter said there wasn't a clear motive, but I didn't care about the papers. I didn't read any of it, not the English papers or the Italian ones. I got my news from Cino.

And more news was coming. I heard his knock on the door, his knock was always the same. Three times, hard. Then he would wait. Then four hard knocks. I answered each time after the four hard knocks. He came in out of breath. I must be ready to go to court tomorrow, he said. Tomorrow? So soon? I thought he meant their trial would be tomorrow. He told me, no. A judge would decide if there was enough evidence to make a charge of murder. It was important, he said. They could be released, or if it went bad, they would go back to the county jail. A terrible place to wait for what would come next, he told me. I didn't know what he meant, a terrible place. I didn't know how it would be otherwise. But then I came to see there were things he was not telling me. What would come next? I asked him. Aspettiamo, he said. We wait. That's all we do. But tomorrow, we go to police court.

The next morning, I rose very early to wake the boys and get them ready. I needed extra time. I wanted us to be washed and well dressed for Ermo, so he would be proud of his family. Cino said the boys must come. It would be important for the judge to see—and for Ermo, too, of course. When Cino came for us in his motorcar, the sun was barely up. He didn't come upstairs, but I saw him there parked on the street wearing goggles for the drive. I quickly picked up Nino and coaxed Aldo down the stairs. We left the house and climbed in the front seat, all four of us there, Nino on my lap. Cino's car had a top but no windows, so I had to wear a scarf. A hat would blow off. I tied the one scarf I had around my head and neck, and we drove north on a dusty road, not like today. It took us about an hour to get there, I'd say. When we pulled up, I couldn't believe my eyes. What a grand building this courthouse in Hartford was. It looked like a castle, a big red brick castle, with many stairs to climb to get in.

Inside, we walked many more stairs to wait in front of the closed doors of the courtroom. Already there were some people waiting to get in, reporters and witnesses, Cino told me, and Frank's people were there, but I told my mother and aunt to stay away. When the guard opened the doors, we walked in and everyone stared at us. Cora was already seated and grunted like a wild pig when we passed. I thought everyone must have heard her. I told Cino, I wanted to sit in the back, but then I changed my mind. I wanted Ermo to see us, so we moved closer to the front. It was a big room. I could see where the judge would sit, above everyone behind a big desk.

When Ermo and Giù were brought in, I almost collapsed, but I had to be strong for them and for the boys, to see their father like that, in chains. It was awful, but I was strong. I smiled for him and blew kisses. I showed him the boys. He smiled back. They sat at a table near to where the judge would sit. They had two lawyers with them. On the other side of the judge was the other table, where another lawyer sat. Then the judge came in and everyone stood until he sat down.

It was terrible. There were so many accusations against them. The lawyer on Frank's side said they did it, that Frank said they did it, from his bed in the hospital the night it happened. Cora said they did it. She cried and pointed at them there with their hands tied and not able to talk back. They could say nothing.

Then the policeman who was there that night said he found a gun that had been fired. I remembered the two policemen leaving with something wrapped in a cloth. I started to stand, to say it wasn't true. They searched twice and didn't find a gun that had been used. There was no gun that had been fired. But Cino pulled me down and told me to be quiet. Why wasn't I allowed to talk? I didn't know. Why did they ask Cora and not me? I could've told them the truth. Then Ermo would be free. But that isn't what happened.

The judge said the state had enough evidence to make them go back to the county jail. He said, 'without bonds.'

I knew what bond was because of the troubles that came to Luigi's followers, those in Milwaukee, I knew to be held without bond meant it was serious. The judge didn't think they were innocent. I broke down when he said this. I covered my face with my hands, the boys on either side were quiet, but I cried. I didn't want people staring at us, but I knew they were. When I looked up, they were taking Ermo and Giù away. I stood and held out my arms, crying. Ermo called to me. Niente paura. he said. Cino, he said, occupati di loro. He didn't want me to worry, and he wanted Cino to care for us. I'm not sure he knew what had happened. His English wasn't so good.

And it was over. They were gone. I couldn't stop crying. We walked out past Cora. I could see the smile on her face. She looked at me and said, 'Butta via la chiave.' Do you know what that means? 'Throw away the key.' I would have strangled her there, but Gino held me back. What makes a woman so evil I wondered as I stared back at her. But I let Cino take us away. I don't know what I would have done without Cino that day. He tried to calm me by telling me everything would be okay. They were innocent, he said. Soon everyone would know. But I didn't know who would believe this. Not after what they heard in that room on that day. Lies, so many lies.

I went home and put the boys in their beds. I went to our room, to our bed, and I lay there until I heard the boys crying for me. It would be another few weeks before I would see Ermo again.

* * *

Finally Cino was coming to pick me up to take me to see this terrible place myself and to see them, my Ermo and Giù. This would've been the end of June.

Jenny came and cared for the boys. She asked if I had family. I told her my mother and my aunt lived not far away. She looked at me as if to ask a question but was quiet. I didn't tell her why I did not see them. My mother had come, the first day. She wanted to bring the priest so he could pray for Ermo and Giù. I lost my mind and told her I would never have a priest in my house. My mother could not understand how I could turn away from the church, especially when I needed prayers. I told her she must never come again to talk to me about religion. And so she left. The last thing she said was that she and my aunt and the priest would pray for us anyway, whether I wanted it or not. I must have slammed the door when she left. I heard her make a noise of surprise.

Jenny didn't say anything, but she kept looking at me. Finally, I told her I didn't want to talk about it. You know how mothers can be, I said, trying to make light of it. But she placed a hand on mine and said sometimes a girl needs her mother. It hit me hard. I pulled my hand away and had to pinch myself until it hurt not to cry. I knew I would think of what she told me, but not then. I was nervous and scared about the car trip to see Ermo and Giù.

It was a hot day when Cino came. Again, he didn't get out of the car, but I saw him waiting, the same goggles, the same coat he had worn when we went to see the judge who made the brothers go back to jail. It was the same long, dusty ride. When we got there and began making our way up the long driveway, I couldn't believe this huge red brick mansion could be the terrible place. It wasn't as grand as the courthouse, but it had a high tower and looked like a place where royalty would live, not prisoners.

Cino parked off to the side of the building. He climbed out and took off the coat he was wearing over his clothes, and I dusted myself off as well as I could. I took off my scarf and tried to smooth my hair. I didn't want Ermo to see me looking a mess.

Walking in, I felt a chill run over my body, even in the heat. The first thing I noticed was the smell, of ammonia and mold. The air was so bad, I thought I would choke on it. I couldn't believe my Ermo was inside this enormous, dark building somewhere. We had to pass by a guard who checked to see that our names were on the list. He searched us and our packages. The food I brought for Ermo and Giù was ruined. Everything was cut through and through with a knife until it spilled over the edge of the tins.

We were questioned by another guard who came to the desk, the same questions again, who have you come to see, have you ever been arrested, do you swear allegiance to the United States. We answered and muttered under our breath. Speak up, he said, and look at me when I talk to you. I didn't want to look at him, afraid he would see my lie. I swore allegiance to no state.

The guard motioned a woman over to take me to another room. My heart began to pound. Where were they taking, I wondered. When we arrived at a small room not far from the desk, the woman guard told me to take off my dress. She touched me everywhere until she was satisfied I didn't have a weapon. She asked me when my baby was due. I didn't answer. Then she insulted me. 'You Italians and your babies,' she said. 'They should send all of you back.' My eyes filled with hot tears, but I wouldn't let her see. It took all my strength not to curse her, la brutta bestia. That's what she was, an ugly beast. By the time we were brought to the room where we would wait for Ermo and Giù, I was near passing out. Cino asked the guard for a glass of water, and they brought it. That was the only kindness I can remember.

Ermo alone was brought to us in shackles. My knees almost gave out when I saw him. He was so thin and pale. He nearly collapsed in my arms. How could this happen in only a few weeks? We cried together and finally Ermo pulled away and dried his eyes. I gave him the food. He could eat it there, but he couldn't take it back. He couldn't give it to Giù.

Ermo ate the mess I gave him as though it were a feast. It was only pieces of lasagna with some meat. They wouldn't let me give him the fork and spoon I brought. They took them away and said I could have them back when we left. He ate with his hands and cleaned himself with the napkin I brought.

He cried that he couldn't give food to Giù. It was not like him to be emotional. He said his brother was not well, and he was worried. They were in cells next to each other but hardly ever saw one another, only when they were allowed a short walk in the sun a few times a week. And he was worried about me and the boys. He held my stomach and asked the baby to forgive him. I couldn't see him like this, blaming himself for everything. It was not his fault, I told him. Don't talk like that. I told him not to worry about us. We were fine. I told him Cino was taking care of everything. He looked at Cino, in the eyes, to make sure it was true.

Then we talked. Cino was with us the whole time. The jail

was a place of torment, Ermo told me. It was always dark, only a dirty little window let in some light. The food was no food at all. Water, a few crumbs, and once a day some soup with nothing in it. I couldn't bear to hear him say these things, but I tried to be cheerful. It didn't work. I couldn't stop the tears from coming. Ermo brushed them away and we cried again together.

I didn't speak all the way home.

That summer was so hot. I worried about Ermo every day and I couldn't see him again. Cino saw them once or twice more but told me there were limits on the number of times people could come, and they needed to save visits for the lawyers. Cino said they were getting ready for court. I asked about Ermo and Giù, were they eating, was Ermo still so pale and thin? He didn't say very much, but I knew it was bad. I was beginning to forget what it was to be a follower of Luigi's. His *Cronoca* was outlawed that summer. It was over, it seemed. Ella was still in prison in Chicago. Augusto had disappeared. And the Sanchinis did not come back. Cino was the only one still out in the open. And I was glad because he was my only link to Ermo and Giù.

Jenny's words stuck with me, about my mother, about needing her. My belly was growing, and I thought about Mamma more and more. One day, I swallowed my pride and went to see her. I left the boys with Jenny and walked to my aunt's. My mother screamed when she saw me. Another baby. I hadn't told her. Oh Lia. What will you do? When she said that, I almost turned to run home. But she wouldn't let me go. She led me to their couch where she and Aunt Abelia took turns petting me and bringing me sweet cookies and milk. I melted into their care. It was good. I wasn't such a good anarchist any longer.

After that, they came to see me and to care for the boys

regularly. I started going out to the market and to the post office where I mailed letters to Ermo. I'm not sure he got them because I never got letters back from him.

I started buying the papers myself. It was always about the war, but on the street, it was busy. When I went to market, I saw people on the sidewalks and in the shops. The papers wrote about business as usual. Everything was about patriotic duty. Factories started making things for the war. The newspapers wrote about boys going off to the front and everything that was going overseas from New Britain, all kinds of parts for guns and bullets and gas masks All kinds of metal, from belt buckles to things like hinges and locks. New Britain was known for these things, but now everything was for the war. And women were working too or home, knitting socks and sweaters. Everyone had to buy bonds. Of course, I hated the war, but I stayed quiet. We all stayed quiet, wherever we were, whoever was left. Our war with the business of war was over. At least then, it seemed over. I was done with all of it, anyway.

I only cared about Ermo and Giù. And about our family. Money was low. My mother helped and Cino. He said I should think about closing the shop, but I wouldn't think of it. We had some customers. Not everyone shunned us for our troubles. Charles opened and closed up every day, and I begged Cino to send over a cobbler friend from Keningston to do whatever repairs needed doing, once or twice a week. It wasn't much, but it helped. I managed to keep things going.

In August, Cino came. He knocked hard on the door, three times, then four, as usual. I knew something must have happened, though. The knocking was louder and more insistent. I let him in. He had a newspaper in his hand. He wanted to know if I had seen it. No, I didn't see it, I told him. Then he showed me, something about the brothers' case happening in September. Was this the trial? I asked him. But no, this was the grand jury. I didn't know what that was. It was to see if they would be indicted for murder. He was growing impatient with me. If they are indicted by the grand jury, there will be a trial. This comes first, he explained. I didn't think I could take any more of this American justice. I was tired of it. My babies needed their father. What is all this? I was getting pazza, crazy, with all this waiting. But wait, that is what we must do. Aspettiamo.

From August to September, this was the longest time. The news was full of death. The boys dying in the war. They died fighting and they were dying of a nfruenza, the flu, they called it, like what Ermo had but so much worse, many more were dying of this sickness than from fighting, but Jenny told me of one of the soldiers she knew who had died in action. He was a high school boy. Jenny knew his parents. They said he wanted to keep the country safe from the Germans, and he was killed there. These parents who lost their sons, she told me, they aren't going to like immigrants who didn't fight. She said this kindly. You must be careful, she said. She was worried for us. I thought then about moving in with my mother and aunt. I thought about closing the shop. I didn't go to my mother's, but business was bad. Cino's cobbler stopped coming. One day I walked downstairs when Charles came. He was turning the sign from closed to open, and I stopped him. Leave it, I said. That was the end of it.

While I was waiting for this grand jury, I worried about Ermo and Giù in jail because the terrible flu was here in New Britain, not just in the hospitals where the soldiers were. People in town were getting sick. People were dying. It was so much worse than Ermo's sickness, and that was so bad, I thought he might die. But with this one, people could die fast. My mother came one day and was shaking from the story of a neighbor, a woman, she wasn't old, she had kids in school, but she was nauseated after dinner. She said it was something she ate, and she was going to complain to the butcher the next day. Then she had a headache, then a fever. She went to bed, but she died the next day. It wasn't the butcher's fault, my mother told me. It was the influenza. They didn't call it the Spanish flu in the early days.

The newspapers wrote about it, but they said, don't panic. It's just the flu. Nature is the cure, they said. No cause for panic. But of course, neighbors knew the truth. The fever was terrible, the cough was like Ermo's but worse. My aunt, who knew a nurse at the New Britain hospital, said the sick drowned from the fluid in their lungs, but first they turned red and purple, their faces and hands and feet. Orribile. And like Jenny, she warned me, they are blaming immigrants. They say we are dirty and spreading germs. We have to be careful, she told me.

Orribile, but my worry was the grand jury, not the flu. Cino told me there was no flu in the jail. One thing to be thankful for.

11
TRA LA PERDUTA GENTE

Hartford
September 1918

T here was not a familiar face in that courtroom, no one to say Erasmo was innocent. No one to say Giù could not kill a man. Returned to the county jail after the grand jury hearing, Erasmo is near tearing his hair. Murder. The brothers were indicted for murder. On the edge of his cot, as far away from the damp wall as possible, he finds no comfort anywhere. Even his clothes rankle, as though touching open wounds. He presses his hands over his ears trying to ignore the rat on the small table against the wall. Sitting in Erasmo's bowl, it's licking the beads of grease remaining from last night's soup. Erasmo wants to smash it with his shoe, but now he must think. He cannot afford to forget the events of this remarkable day. He must make some sense of it.

The attorney Erasmo had never seen, who was against them, pointed to a display of guns and knives. The policeman Erasmo did not know who had been in his house the night he and Giù were arrested was there in the courtroom, before the judge, telling terrible lies about them. The large gun, the policeman said, was found wrapped in a cloth in the basement. He said it was Erasmo's, but Erasmo had no such large gun. His own were the two small ones on the table. These were not guns to kill a man; one was broken. But the policeman spoke only of the large gun. He told the judge and the jury it had been fired the night Frank was shot and stabbed. Erasmo could have told the judge and the jury that there was no such gun in his basement. Erasmo had never seen that gun. And they accused Giù of using the large knife to cut Frank's face and neck, which could never be, because Giù would never inflict such injuries on any living creature, much less a man. That knife was from his kitchen. Lia used it to cut chicken for cooking.

And where were the nurses who were in the hospital, who knew Frank never said 'Erasmo shot me' and 'Giuseppe cut me'? They would never say these things because these lies were not true. Is that why they were not there, why no one who knew the truth was there? Why was the beat policeman, who had been in his house, Dolan, why was he not there? He told Erasmo not to worry. He knew the truth, but where was Dolan?

After the police and their false evidence and the lies, the judge asked Erasmo and Giù if they had anything more to add, but of course Giù could add nothing. He hardly understood what had been said. Erasmo understood. He knew they were being falsely accused. He could not understand why, but he knew the words. Why didn't he speak? His English. It was not good, and he did not want to appear stupid in front of those educated Americans: the judge, the lawyers, and the jury. Now he thinks he made a mistake. But there was still the trial to come. That's when the truth had to be told, at the trial.

He had to think straight, to tell the lawyers, this Noble Pierce and the other named McDonough, every true detail.

They must set it right for the trial. He would go over it again and again. How much time had passed? He did not know. It is easy to lose track of time in the darkness of his cell. But it must still be day. The light bulb hanging over the small table in the corner was allowed only at night, and it's not on. The rat is gone, or hiding. Never mind, Erasmo must think.

He tries to remember all the details on the night of his arrest, being torn from his bed, his home, his wife and babies. Before being pushed into the back of the police wagon, Erasmo had looked up to see the light on in his home, upstairs where Lia was with the boys. When would he see them again? He looked over at Giù who was folded into himself, half a man. No words passed between them on the way to the hospital. When they stopped, Carlson opened the door to lead the brothers, handcuffed, out of the wagon. Barely securing their footing, they were pushed up the stairs of the red brick hospital on Grand. Erasmo was in a daze at the hospital. He and Giù were led into a dimly lit space in the corridor. Carlson removed the cuffs and told them not to get any ideas. The policeman, who Erasmo did not know, would keep watch.

He has a gun and knows how to use it, Carlson said before leaving them there and going out the way they had come in.

He and Giù were told to sit in the two wood chairs outside the room where Frank was lying. Erasmo could see through the door to the bed. He could not tell if Frank was conscious. Soon a doctor appeared from the room and motioned to the policemen to bring them in. In the room there was the doctor who was examining Frank and also two young nurses, all in white and very clean. Frank had bandages covering one side of his face and around his neck, but he would receive good care in this place, Erasmo thought. Surely, he will recover.

Frank began to gesture toward them. He was weak, but he was awake and moving. Seeing him pointing toward Erasmo and Giù, the doctor leaned over Frank. Do you know these two men? he asked. And Frank said yes. He wanted to know if Frank knew their names, and Frank said yes. They are Erasmo and Giuseppe, he said. Did they do this to you? And Frank said no. Then the doctor asked if he had any trouble with the brothers and Frank again said no. The doctor seemed disturbed by these answers. And asked the same questions over again until Frank grew confused. At one point he said yes, but it was clear he was by now not sure what question he was answering.

Erasmo noticed the nurses exchanging looks with one another, as though they were troubled by the questions and thought maybe Frank could not keep it all straight in his head.

By this time, Erasmo was getting worried and having trouble controlling his anger. It would not be good to be angry now, but still he knew he must speak.

You are not lying there saying we did this to you, he said to Frank. Tell them the truth.

He spoke this to Frank in Italian. But before Frank could answer, the doctor stopped them both from speaking. There will be none of that, he said, and he motioned the policeman to take Erasmo and Giù back to the corridor.

I want a lawyer, Erasmo said, as he was led out of the room.

You want a lawyer, do you? Well don't you worry. You'll get justice.

When the doctor said this, Erasmo looked over his shoulder at him. That's when he saw the expression confirming his suspicions. Erasmo knew mockery when he heard it and when he saw it, un sorrisetto. He would like to wipe that look off his face. This was the look of disrespect, when one man does not respect another.

He and Giù talked quietly to each other in the corridor, Erasmo trying to calm Giù, telling him the truth would come out and not to worry. Giù said it was very strange that the doctor wanted Frank to accuse them. Why would he do that? he asked. After some minutes, Erasmo wasn't sure how much time had passed, they were brought back to Frank's bed. A policeman who was Italian followed them in. The doctor said this Italian policeman would be the translator. The doctor said it will be better this way. You may speak in your language, and this policeman, who is one of you, will tell me what is said. That way there is no mistaking. You will clearly understand. So now, Mr. Palmese, please answer the interpreter's questions.

Erasmo watched as the doctor sat in the chair by the bed, his hands behind his head.

The policeman asked the same questions. Did Frank know them? He said yes. Did these men shoot you and cut you? Frank said no. Did you have trouble with them? Frank said no. Then the policeman asked Frank if he had trouble with anyone. And Frank looked at him.

You're Italian, so you know. If you're Italian, out on the street, that is enough, Frank said.

The policeman nodded. And it was true, certainly for Frank. He always had problems. He was always in trouble with someone. He did not tell the interpreter or the doctor that Erasmo had trouble with his sister, Cora. Erasmo knew it was best not to say anything about that, but Erasmo remembered. He could have struck Cora when she was rough with Lia on the stairs at her aunt's apartment. He wanted to. But it is good that Frank did not mention that time.

Erasmo waited for the policeman to tell the doctor what Frank had said. He thought surely now they will let him and Giù go back home, now it was clear Frank did not accuse them. Erasmo even thought Frank might recover. He didn't seem so bad. He looked at Giù and smiled who smiled back. Erasmo even smiled at Frank. Grazie, he said. But the policeman did not tell the doctor what Frank had said. Instead, the doctor made the policeman who kept watch over the brothers take them back outside.

They waited out there for a long time. Then another doctor came and Erasmo heard him tell the doctor who examined Frank that the surgery room was available. They were going to take Frank to surgery.

Hearing this, Erasmo stood in the doorway. What about us? he asked.

Frank's doctor looked up from the bed and asked in return, What about you? Why, you're going to jail.

The policeman who kept guard handcuffed him and then Giù again. Erasmo saw Carlson coming back up the corridor.

But Frank said we didn't do it, Erasmo said.

The doctor looked at Erasmo. You are confused, son. And now we have to go, or the charge of deadly assault might become one of murder. Please move. You're in the way.

With his hands now cuffed, which was a good thing, Erasmo could not do what he wanted to do. Giù looked at Erasmo. Calma, he said.

Out on the sidewalk, Erasmo saw sunlight beginning to stream into the large window of the hospital. It was first light, and he could see the two doctors wheeling Frank into the surgery room that faced the street. Jostled once again into the police wagon, the two brothers were driven away, on their way to the county jail.

The night of the arrest, the hospital, the grand jury, all part of the nightmare that would not end. Erasmo is tired and can think no more. He lies down on the cot and pulls up the thin, grey blanket. He draws his legs to his chest. What time is it? It doesn't matter. He falls into a shallow sleep.

* * *

After the grand jury, Cino came alone and was able to see Erasmo and Giù in jail, in the same room where Lia had been, when she brought him food and they had cried together. It was a terrible time. And yet there had been hope that their innocence would be revealed, but that hope seemed to be growing dimmer. There was still the trial. Another chance.

Cino was nervous, Erasmo thought. He asked what was wrong, but Cino shook his head and said nothing was wrong. He didn't like seeing them there, but no, there was nothing wrong. He hoped that after the trial they would be together again in Cino's yard drinking wine and saluting their courtroom victory. But he said this without belief, it seemed to Erasmo. Cino told them that Lia and the boys were well. Erasmo asked about the pregnancy and Cino said it was good. Lia and the baby were growing, in good health he said. Then he said they were raising money for their lawyers. Many dollars were coming in, he said. Cino talked to whoever was around to talk to and he made an ad for the Italian newspaper. Don't worry, he said. The money is coming in. It will be there to pay Noble Pierce and this Patrick McDonough.

Then Giù, who had remained silent, spoke. Why is it, Cino, he asked, that you alone are free to come and go as you please? Why are you not out of sight like the rest of your followers?

This seemed to cause Cino some pain. He began to tap his fingertips together in front of his chest, his breaths coming in short bursts. But perhaps his anguish was anger, because he soon spoke harshly to Giù.

Are you questioning me? he asked. Me, who takes care of the family, who brings you news, who hired your lawyers? Who works day and night to make sure you will be free?

Giù drew back and lowered his head but did not apologize. He let his question and Cino's response hang in the air between them. But Erasmo, thinking of Cino's words, knew they could not afford Cino's anger. He was doing all the things he said, and the brothers needed him. There was no one else. So Erasmo spoke.

Sì, cousin, he began. All you say is true. We thank you for all you do. We are glad you are free to help us.

Cino was beginning to calm down, but the mention of his freedom caused him to look sharply at Erasmo. He said nothing.

Erasmo continued to explain. It's my brother's illness. Do not be too hard on him. It is only that he wants to have a decent bowl of soup and to lie down in a comfortable bed. It's nothing.

They both looked at Giù who slowly nodded. He would say no more. Cino was satisfied and that was the end of it.

After their cousin left and Erasmo and Giù were led back to their cells, Erasmo looked up at the sliver of light from the narrow window filmed with dirt. The light, scant as it was, made him uneasy. He pictured Cino out in it, driving his car in his coat, his goggles protecting his vision, like a rich man, he thought. A rich, free man. This image, so distant from the Beautiful Idea, the one they all shared, Luigi, the Sanchinis, little Ella, his Lia, Cino. What happened? He continued, lost in thought, looking toward the sun he knew was out there. Cino, a rich man. It was confounding. He shook his head, but it could yet be okay, if Cino held the key to their freedom. The last thing he told them, the trial date was firm. October 1, 1918.

12
THE TRIALS OF THE LIVING

New Britain
July 20, 1995

After the grand jury, I wouldn't see Ermo again until the trial. The horror of this time was something I couldn't have imagined. It was only a few years earlier that he had seen me in his shop, had wanted to marry me. He said when he saw me skipping from his shop after leaving off my father's shoes, he knew I would soon be old enough to be his wife. He knew it even then. And I knew it, too. I knew when I saw him at the Sanchinis'. I knew it when I wouldn't let my father keep us apart. And we were happy in our own place. Ermo was proud of what he owned in the new country. He always wanted a home and a wife and children. And he had them. We were happy.

When I think back on it, I wonder sometimes why we were so committed to the Idea. We had everything, and yet we wanted more, not just for us, no, a better world for everyone. Was I the cause of our troubles? I had to convince Ermo to join us in the cause. He didn't want to, not at first. Not that he didn't know it was true, the injustice and corruption of the powerful. No, he knew it. But he always knew it and knew it always would be so. A small mouse cannot kill the cat, no matter what we tell ourselves. He said that to me more than once. Then, fece spallucce. That's what he did, shrug his shoulders, over things that could not be changed. Even so, we tried. Because it was a worthy fight.

But look what it brought. Except for Cino, everyone was gone, in hiding somewhere. The month of Ermo and Giù's trial, the government made us illegal. It did. If you were known to follow Luigi, you would be deported. The Sanchinis didn't come back to their home in New Britain, still in hiding somewhere. And Ella, poor Ella. She was indicted in October. Her trial was the same month as the brothers. All anyone cared about was would she talk. But she didn't, and so she was a hero. But she was a child. A child put on a train with dynamite.

Was it my fault that Ermo and Giù would pay the price for our beliefs? I will ask myself that question until I die. Some newspapers said the brothers had 'anarchistic tendencies.' What did that mean? What were they implying, and where was the evidence? Was it because we were Italian? Is that all it took to be considered the enemy in this country? Why were they spreading these suspicions? If the police had known about the deeds, the fires, the flyers that blanketed the city, wouldn't they have arrested Ermo then? And there was nothing to connect Giù to any of it, so how was he an anarchist at all? And yet the newspapers said it, and so everyone believed it to be true.

But even today, ask me what I believe and I will tell you: I believe in the Beautiful Idea, as far away from possible as it is.

Cino was the only one of us who was living freely, but he had stopped his meetings and published no more flyers, and he carried out no more deeds. He ran his business as a respectable man. It got under my skin, I tell you. I didn't understand it, but he was the only one who intervened for the brothers. He collected money for their defense. He talked to the lawyers, and, most of all, he looked after us. Always asking did we need anything or could he do anything? And he was a savior for us, for me and the boys, really, a little money here, some groceries there. But mainly because he went to see them when my belly was growing and brought me news of my Ermo and Giù in that terrible place.

I'm putting it off, but now I have to tell you about the trial. It is a hard memory, and I don't talk about these things, you know. I don't speak of it any longer to my own Amalia, but I said I would tell you, and I will.

October 1, 1918, an unusually warm day. I remember it well after all these years. That first day, my mother came to care for the boys. Cino picked me up as he had done, and we drove in his Buick to Hartford, to the county courthouse. All the government buildings in those days were bigger and grander than any other buildings around it. I think it was because Americans didn't have castles and palaces, so they built big government buildings to make up for it. To show where the power was. I remember craning my neck to look at how tall it was, four or five stories high. We had been there before, but today it made me shake. This is when I began to have questions. All this grandeur to accuse two immigrants for killing another. I didn't think the government cared a bit about these men. No, I thought, maybe this is about something else.

I saw Cora there, outside, before we went in. I heard her telling friends in a loud voice that Frank was always in trouble with someone over something. Then she saw me and turned away, lowering her voice.

Inside, the courtroom was also grand. In the front was a

platform, like a stage, and a high desk, above everyone else. That was where the judge sat. Below him, on the right side was the witness box, where I would be called up. Across from there were the rows of seats for the jury. In the middle, facing the judge, was a long table for the lawyers and the accused. Behind them there was a railing separating these court people from the witnesses who would be called up to testify and the people who came to look—family, friends, and the curious. In the middle of the ceiling was a big electric fan with four blades to keep the room cool. It was hot in there. I remember that. The whole building had electricity, a lot of buildings did then. Even houses were getting it. Ermo said we would too, in time. I would live to see that day, but not with my Ermo.

We walked to the front and sat behind the railing as soon as the doors were opened. I wanted Ermo and Giù to see us, Cino and me, to know they could look at us and see that we would always be there. I remember being startled when the man in the front, the bailiff, said for us to all rise. He said, 'Hear ye, hear ye, all rise.'

I never forgot that, they really say it. That's when the judge came in. Lucien Burpee. And the lawyer against us, Hugh Alcorn. Our lawyer was Noble Pierce. A good man. Maybe not a strong one, but he tried. Then they brought in Ermo and Giù, handcuffed. I looked and looked to get their attention. Finally Ermo looked back at me and smiled. I tried to smile too, but it was through my tears. I didn't want him to see me cry. How thin he was and so pale. No matter how much food I sent to him through Cino, my Ermo must have shivered it all away in that terrible place.

That first day was about the lies they said before. And the doctor who was in the hospital when Frank died, he was there, Dr. Elcock, a mean man who only wanted the brothers to be pronounced guilty. Everything he said was a lie. You can read about it in the papers, what he said. He said Frank understood English perfectly. Well, I can tell you, his English was not so good. We, all of us, we always spoke Italian. That's the language we knew best. But that doctor, he said Frank knew English as well as he did. That was a lie. He also said Frank accused Ermo and Giù, but Cino knew better, because Ermo told him the truth about the hospital. Frank never said that. I wanted to stand and scream, liar, but Cino told me, calma.

Noble Pierce rose and objected many times, because of what the doctor said, but then the other one, Alcorn, he just said the same thing a different way until the judge let it go. That doctor lied about other things, about the Italian policeman interpreter. Ermo knew what Frank really said. All during this time, Erasmo looked at us. He knew they were lying, but what could he do. Fece Spallucce. That's what he did. I started to cry, but I had to stop myself.

The lawyer for Frank and the doctor kept saying over and over that Frank knew he was going to die. But Ermo told Cino Frank didn't look like he was going to die. He didn't act like he was going to die. He never said he was going to die, the way the doctor said.

On and on it went, again about guns and knives, especially the gun that was not Ermo's, that the policeman found. But he never found that gun in our house. That gun was put there. Why, I asked myself, why were they doing this? Why these lies? They said they dug Frank up and cut out his hip bone. They brought it into the courtroom to show everyone. They talked about how the bullet went in this way and came out that way, but none of this had anything to do with Ermo and Giù, but how Cora screamed and cried when she saw that. The judge banged the gavel. The bailiff said we had to take a break.

It was so hot in there, even with the fan. We went outside to get some fresh air. I was sweating and had to pull my hair back and away from my neck. I was wearing a summer dress over my belly. It was tight from the heat and sticking to me. I knew that the people near us from inside the courtroom were looking and could see we were having a baby, Ermo and me. Good, I thought. Let them see. Let them see that my babies are without their father. Soon we were called back in.

And then they called Cora up for questioning. I could see how nervous she was. She nearly stumbled up to the witness box. She wasn't pretty in any way. She had short black hair around her big face. She was stout with square legs. And worse, now her face was red and wet with sweat. She had a handkerchief that she was wringing between both hands. She was a mess. I did not feel sorry for her.

Then Alcorn asked her if there had ever been trouble between her brother Frank and the brothers on trial, and she said yes. There was an argument, and she pointed to Erasmo. She said he slapped her three times, and when Frank, he tried to stop him, Erasmo said to Frank, 'I don't forget. If it is not one day, it will be another. I'm going to do it to you.' Then she pointed at Ermo and Giù and said, 'They did it; they killed him.'

This was terrible, all lies. I let out a little scream. I remember I could not stand it anymore. Cino leaned over and whispered in my ear. It's okay, he said because you will be a witness next. And it was true I would be. My time was coming. I had met with Noble Pierce and Patrick McDonough, the other attorney, in their office in Hartford before the trial. They told me what questions I would be asked and what I should say. And I knew these were all lies, what Cora was saying.

Noble Piere asked Cora if it wasn't true that Frank had some trouble, a fight, three weeks before he died, and she said who told you that? Whoever said that, they are false witnesses, she said.

False witness? She was the false witness. Even the papers said that Frank was in a fight.

Cora stepped down and gave me a smirk. But I didn't do anything, because as soon as she passed, I was called. My heart was pounding, I was nervous, and when I rose to walk to my place, I looked at Ermo. We exchanged looks of our love for each other. I remember hearing people talking under their breath. It was my summer dress and my belly. And I have to tell you, in those days, I was the opposite of Cora Necchi.

The questions from Noble Pierce went as I expected. I was able to say that Ermo and I and the boys had been home all night and that we were asleep when Frank was next door lying in Cora's yard. I said it was true that we were asleep and knew of nothing until the police came pounding on our door. Then he questioned me about what Cora said.

There was no trouble between Frank and Erasmo and Giuseppe, I said. That argument Cora talks about, is about when I was pregnant with Nino and she grabbed me and pulled my hair, and almost pushed me down the stairs. Erasmo pushed her away from me. Frank wasn't even there, he was downstairs, but he had nothing to do with it. No, she is our next-door neighbor, but we do not talk to her, or go to her parties. Our trouble was not with Frank.

I said all that and again there was murmuring in the courtroom. That's when Cora got up and said I was lying. The judge banged the gavel and told her to sit down. I don't think anyone believed her, anyway. I thought I did a good job up there. Then Alcorn got up to question me. I thought I was ready for him. But he asked me only one question.

Mrs. Perretta, he said, Is it not true that a good and loving wife will lie for her husband?

Noble Pierce objected, and Alcorn said he had no further questions. I was told to step down, but first I looked that lawyer in the eye, and I said, loud enough for all to hear, I'm a wife who does not lie. That was all. I went back to sit by Cino.

Then came the witnesses.

Of all those called up to testify, who heard shots and saw two men running away from the scene that night, no one said it was Ermo and Giù. One witness said she saw two men running by her house. She said they had dark suits and one of the men was big and heavy. Ermo and Giù did not have dark suits, and the brothers were not big and heavy.

And then I saw Charles. He testified. And now I knew why he and Jenny thought the brothers were innocent. He saw two men standing near where the murder took place, a little after twelve o'clock that night. One of the men was stocky, not like Erasmo. He said he knew Erasmo, and it wasn't him. He said he was out walking, on his way home. The two men he saw were right where it happened. I was so happy. I could have kissed him. I thought with these witnesses, it was clear. The brothers didn't do it. I thought we would all go home.

But, what's the use? It went on for two more days after that, with more and more lies until the truth was lost. You know how it ended.

I am so tired now. I think that is all.

13

IL DOLOROSO REGNO

Hartford, Connecticut
October 1918

T he trial, the last chance for the truth. Erasmo is quaking
in his cell. The trial is not going well, he knows this. His
attorney says it is, but Erasmo knows better. The same lies, the
hospital, Frank's own words distorted. The guns and knives.
All of it wrong. And Dolan, now he discovers, Dolan, who was
present during the first search of his house, could not testify
because he was now suddenly in the war and at sea. How could
this be? Why is he not there to say this, the truth, that Erasmo
and Giù were not hiding on the street somewhere waiting to
kill Frank?

Lia, beautiful Lia, she told the truth on the first day, in
good, strong English. But what good would her words do? She
told that lawyer, Alcorn, to his face, that she does not lie. And it
is true. She does not lie.

Today, the trial's second day, Erasmo and Giù each were
called to the witness stand to defend themselves. Poor Giù, so

sick, he could hardly speak. Lia must have been shocked to see him, so thin. And his English. Erasmo thinks he does not understand. How can he defend himself? But he was good. Erasmo told his brother in the courtroom, bene, brother, he said.

Giù explained that he was in bed and didn't hear any noises until his brother got him up. He had no trouble with Frank Palmese. He explained about the knives, the big kitchen knife, he never takes it out of the kitchen, he told them. He told the truth, he heard no screams. He did not cut and stab Frank.

* * *

Erasmo had a better time of it, he thinks. His English was good. He began in a low voice, but it grew stronger.

He told them, I am a shoemaker; I polish and repair shoes. I live and work on Cherry Street. I am in New Britain, I bought my property, soon, two years ago—Amalia and me, we marry and have two sons. We have another baby in the spring.

He remembers then, just then, clearing his throat and speaking louder. The night of the murder, when Frank is killed, I am in bed. Amelia and me, we go to sleep while they are singing next door. Then, I wake up because of policemen banging on my door. I never see the big revolver before. It is not mine. I do not know how it got in my basement.

When Noble Peirce asked him, Mr. Perretta, Erasmo, did you kill Frank Palmese? Erasmo shook his head, slowly but surely.

No. I have no trouble with Frank. I did not shoot him. We did not do it.

He did well, but now in his cell, he is not so sure. Why didn't Noble Pierce ask him about the lies? I could have told them about the hospital, but Noble Pierce did not let me speak about the hospital. He is a good man, but I think he is letting me, us, down, Erasmo thinks.

Erasmo will not sleep this night, he knows. Tomorrow they will go back to the courtroom. Maybe then he will be able to tell them about all the lies, about Dolan, the gun, the hospital. But this thought does not help. He does not sleep.

* * *

The next day, the judge says the trial is over, no more witnesses. Now is the time for final arguments, he said. But Erasmo is shaking his head. There is not much more to be said. He hasn't had his chance to expose all the lies.

Now instead of talk, Erasmo must listen to Alcorn, and what he hears alarms him so much that Noble Pierce has to put his hand on his arm and squeeze. It is a warning. He had told Erasmo many times that he must be a calm man, not a man who is roused to anger. Such a man might be a murderer. But Erasmo is not a murderer. Who would not be alarmed by lies with no chance to tell the truth?

But Alcorn told the lies again and again. Again he shames Lia. Of course a wife lies for her husband, he says. Again he puts false words in the mouth of Frank Palmese, who can no longer tell them what happened on that night.

We must remember the feud between the two families, he says.

But there was no feud, only Cora Necchi's lies.

And what did Alcorn mean when he said, There are a lot of things we haven't referred to—Oh, a whole lot of things.

What things? He must tell what those things are. Does the jury know? Why don't we know? Erasmo is at war in his mind, trying to understand and trying to be calm so Noble Pierce won't be troubled. Erasmo must sit quietly and listen when this evil, lying man tells the jury that he and Giù have guns and knives and are murderers.

But we do not have murder weapons, only a small gun, one broken, and a kitchen knife never taken out of the kitchen. Who could believe these false words?

But now this Alcorn says that we must be found guilty of murder in the first degree. Erasmo is angry and confused, not sure what he is hearing. Surely the jury knows they are not murderers. Both he and Giù told everyone from the first day that they are innocent.

Erasmo begins to calm down when Noble Pierce stands. He is a noble man, tall and straight, with the white hair of age and wisdom. Surely, the jury will listen to him.

Noble Pierce tells them that Erasmo Perretta is no murderer. He is a family man with a home and a business, just as Erasmo told them. He tells the jury things about the guns. Erasmo cannot follow the argument, but his words are strong, and Erasmo is sure the jury will know that the big gun was not his. Erasmo knows that Noble Pierce is telling the jury that there was no time for the brothers to have done these terrible things and to be in their beds by the time the police came banging. He thinks he hears Noble Pierce mention Dolan. He hopes so because Erasmo told him many times what Dolan said and that he knew Erasmo was innocent. And the witnesses, too, who said they saw people who were not Erasmo and Giù. Noble Pierce says their names. He says other things too, not to let prejudice get in the way. Erasmo knows this word. He knows Italians are not trusted or believed. Noble Pierce tells the jury to think hard on these doubts. Erasmo knows the term reasonable doubt. He knows any reasonable man would have doubts about all they have heard.

And the noble Noble Pierce asks if they think their consciences will be clear if these men are sent to their deaths.

Erasmo understands most of this, and he wants to thank Noble Pierce for being honest and telling the jury they have heard only lies from the dishonest lawyer, Alcorn. But Pierce shakes his head, as if to say, Don't say anything. So Erasmo turns to Giù beside him and smiles. But it doesn't appear that Giù has understood any of it.

Lucien Burpee tells the jury they have heard and must pay attention to all the evidence. He bangs his gavel, and the court sergeant leads the jury out of the courtroom.

Erasmo and Giù want to talk to Noble Pierce, but he has left. They are handcuffed and taken to the bathroom with armed guards. After, they are shackled again and led to a small room next to the courtroom where they sit in hard, straight chairs while the armed guards stand over them.

Before long, they are led back to their seats to sit by Noble Pierce. It didn't take very long, Erasmo thinks, when the jury returns. They must all agree that the brothers are innocent. That is why they did not take very long. He looks to Noble Pierce for a nod of his head, to indicate, yes, this is a good sign, but Pierce stares straight ahead and does not look at Erasmo. Erasmo looks at Giù, in his own world, far away. What must he be thinking? Erasmo looks at the judge as he adjusts his robes and sits down, high above them.

Lucien Burpee asks, Does the jury have a verdict?

And a man stands up and says, Yes, we have, your Honor.

The next words fly fast.

What say you?

Guilty, your Honor.

Erasmo hears these words, but does not know if it can be true. He hears Amalia cry out. His eyes go to her. He sees her fall back in her chair. He sees Cino put his arm around her and try to comfort her. Erasmo doesn't like this. He is worried about

Amalia and the baby. He tries to stand, but a guard pushes him back down.

Erasmo turns to look at Giù. His eyes are questioning. Colpevoli, Erasmo tells him. They say we are guilty.

Giù crumples. His hand comes up to cover his mouth. Erasmo looks again toward Amalia. He catches her eye. She is crying and wiping her face with her bare hands. He is at a loss and shrugs his shoulders. Fece Spallucce. What can be done? He is helpless to help.

There is noise and confusion in the courtroom. Erasmo sees Cora Necchi with a look of great satisfaction on her face. Erasmo is not a murderer and he did not kill Frank Palmese, but if he could jump over the chairs and the railing, he just might strangle Cora until that look on her face vanished. He has to turn away.

Lucien Burpee bangs his gavel once more. He commands order. He says, 'Thank you, gentlemen of the jury, for a verdict that is quite proper in the eyes of the Court.'

These words Erasmo understands. But he does not understand how a judge could say them.

You are dismissed, he tells the jury.

They scatter quickly, never looking the brothers in the eye.

Lucien Burpee asks the brothers to step forward.

Erasmo and Giù stand before him.

Do you have anything to say before the Court passes judgment?

Erasmo and Joseph mumble no under their breaths and shake their lowered heads.

Lucien Burpee says many things Erasmo does not understand about the Court and their guilt and the sheriff of Hartford who will take them to the state prison in Wethersfield. He mentions a day and an hour. And then he says something both he and Giù clearly understand. That they will each be hanged by the neck until dead. He bangs the gavel so hard, Erasmo and Giù jump.

Lucien Burpee pays them no mind. He says, This case is now concluded.

Erasmo and Joseph each stumble against the arms of the guards by their sides.

Amalia screams out, but Erasmo is not able to think of her at this moment.

14
DAYS OF DARKNESS AND LIGHT

New Britain, Connecticut
July 27, 1995

I remember the days after the trial like seeing in the dark. I stayed in our bedroom, Ermo's and mine. I kept the curtains closed against the light. I didn't know if it was day or night. Mamma and Aunt Abelia came every day to care for me and the boys. I lost interest in my children, even the unborn one. My baby was growing inside me, but I was withering. My mother tried to feed me pastas with cheese and cream, but I couldn't stomach such things. Only soup with noodles, that was all I could manage. Mamma fed me from a spoon, like a baby. Then when she thought I was calm, she talked to me of God. When she did this, I turned to the wall. One day she said she would call the priest if I didn't get up and take care of the babies. I warned her against it.

Why a priest? I asked. Am I dying?

You need the priest, because you need God's love, she said.

God's love? If there was such a thing as 'God's love,' there would never have been this nightmare. Where was God and his love when all those lies were heaped upon us, when the evil lawyer and that judge ruined our lives?

She knew I meant it, that I would lock the door to that priest and to her. She dropped it.

The worst was in the cold of November, when the war was over. In the middle of the night the church bells were ringing and factory whistles were blowing. At first, I didn't know what was happening. There were even guns going off. It kept up all night and into the day. I could hear a parade that was over on Main.

Later in the day, Jenny knocked on the door to see if I was all right. I let her in even though I wasn't properly dressed. I had nothing to offer her. She looked around and asked if she could help me put things away. I wasn't even embarrassed for the mess. I told her as long as I could take care of Aldo and Nino things were not so bad. As long as my mother and Aunt Abelia came to help me. I think she could see that if it were not for my mamma and zia, the children would not be cared for.

She asked if she could sit with me, to give me some company, while I waited for them. My mother probably told her to do this. But I didn't mind. Jenny and Charley had been good to us. Charley tried to save Ermo and Giù by telling the truth during the trial. I pointed to the couch. We sat and she told me about the noise and the celebrations.

She and Charley had been with a big group of people in Walnut Hill Park. She said hundreds filled the lawn and spaces all around. The mayor and preachers and other government people gave speeches. Everyone beside themselves with joy. Of course she said every speaker, religious or not, prayed for the boys who wouldn't be coming home. There was great sadness mixed with the joy. So many dead. She stopped as soon as she said it because she knew how I would take it. I held back my tears.

What could I say, that for every torment suffered in the war, Ermo and Giù were suffering as much or more? Rats? They had them. And lice, and dampness, and no comfortable place to rest, food that was not food at all. Could I tell her that they too suffered with death hanging over them every day? All for what? A murder they did not commit? They were taken from me and our babies without a choice, Ermo never to see his sons become men, never to be safe at home again? What a hell this was, as much as for any soldier. But how could I say such things to Americans who believed in war and that every boy who died in one was a hero? No, I couldn't say what I knew was true, that all those who died in this war were fooled by false words.

This was my thinking, you see. The darkness of November and the months ahead would be very bad. The flu was still killing people, and all those who were happy the war was over had to deal with the wounded and the sick. So many had terrible wounds, so many losses—arms, legs, eyes, half faces everywhere. I was sorry for them, but at the same time I was angry because of Ermo and Giù who also suffered. At least for the soldiers, their war was over. Not us. Ours went on.

Cino stopped by during those days to tell me about Ermo and Giù in Wethersfield. When can I go? I asked him over and over.

And he looked at me and said you cannot, you are not well enough. It is a big, and he was sorry to say, terrible place. As terrible as the prison in Hartford but much bigger.

I was like a crazy person because time was running out. They were to be hanged in February, and our baby was due in February. I told Cino, no matter what, I must see them.

Soon, on another visit to me, he had some good news.

Noble Pierce and Patrick McDonough had filed an appeal, and the brothers would not be executed on February 5, as the judge had said in October. I was beside myself with hope. Now I could be happy like the wives whose husbands did not die in the war. My Ermo would not die. Cino let me have this moment, but soon he brought me back to earth. The brothers were still in the war and still fighting for their lives. We must win the appeal, he told me.

When I was calm again, he brought me more news, not good for our gruppo. Ella was sent to prison in November, to the State Penitentiary in Jefferson City. She was there with others like us, Cino told me. Emma Goldman and later, a woman named Kate Richards O'Hare. Cino said they were not like Luigi's followers, but also enemies of the corrupt state. They fought against the same things we did. The conditions were very bad for us and for all those fighting for freedom, he told me. All the while Cino continued to be free, never calling attention to himself, going about his business. And his business had nothing to do with anarchy, it seemed.

How I got through those days and months, I don't know. I refused to go to Thanksgiving, a foolish holiday. What was there to be thankful for in a country where the rich had everything? I, and the boys, were barely hanging on. Cino collected donations for us from the Italians who read about us in the newspapers. And my mother made the priest take a collection for us. There was no reason why her child and the babies should suffer, she told him, and he finally agreed to do it. But I wouldn't take the church money, not at first. Finally, I had to. When we needed charity, but I cursed every cent.

I wouldn't celebrate Christmas, either. This made my

mother and Aunt Abelia sad, so I finally let them take Aldo and Nino on Christmas Eve. I know they took them to mass, but what could I do? I was weak and had to give in to a mother and aunt who loved us and cared for us during these horrible days.

On New Year's Eve, when I heard the bells from South Church at midnight, I sat up alone in our dark bedroom, remembering just one year ago when Ermo sang, *Tramontate, stelle! All'alba vincerò! Vincerò! Vincerò!* Where was victory now? He had such a beautiful voice. My insides froze when I thought I would never hear him sing again.

* * *

February fifth came and went and Ermo and Giù were still alive. Cino continued to bring me word. They were weary, but still they had hope, he told me.

They believe the appeal will save them, he said. Giù, though, had been sick and in the infirmary. When he recovered and returned to his cell, he told Cino, Better to have died in a clean bed than to be back in this terrible place.

As soon as Cino said this, he realized I would take it hard and quickly added, But he is better. In better spirits.

I had to believe that, or I would go mad with so much worry about the two of them. Ermo, he said, was always the stronger one. My Ermo was sad of course but not without hope. I too had some hope, then anyway.

The end of February brought some light into our days. My Amalia was born. When my pain started, Mamma went to the store across the street and demanded to use the phone. Cino came and they got me to the hospital. Aunt Abelia stayed with the boys. At first I didn't want to go to the place where the lying doctor had said such terrible things about Ermo and Giù. But in the end, I went. My mother insisted.

The hospital is modern and clean with doctors and good nurses, she said.

You can't stay here. You must go, she said. I am too old and your zia, too, too old to help you have the baby at home.

And so I went. I don't remember much about the delivery. They took me on a stretcher to a big room and onto a table. I was screaming and telling them I didn't want medicine. I didn't trust American doctors the way my mother did. They gave me something anyway, to put me to sleep. When I woke up I was in a long room with many beds. The maternity ward had two rows of beds spaced apart and facing each other. The center was wide enough for the nurses to roll carts in and out. I was near the door. There were only a few of us in this big place because the husbands hadn't been home from the war long enough yet, and so many were not well.

My mother was right about the nurses. They wore spotless white dresses. Their hair was tied back under big white caps. The one who brought Amalia to me smiled with kindness. Her name was Anna. I think the nurses all knew each other and talked, no matter where in the hospital they were. She told me she knew my husband was away. That is how she said it. Her smile vanished. She looked so sad when she gave Amalia to me.

Look how beautiful she is, she said.

I cried then and didn't stop. The nurses, there were three, each said I had to stop. They were afraid my milk wouldn't come. Mamma told them to give me birra.

Beer? They asked. They were shocked at the idea. But Mamma carried a bottle in and when the nurses were gone, she poured some in a glass and made me drink. The three nurses never knew, but I had milk for my daughter.

Oh how I missed Ermo, each time they brought Amalia to me. A daughter. He would love his daughter, and I didn't know when he would see her. That thought always brought tears.

In those days, the priests came to tell the mothers their duty. When Anna told me a priest was coming, I said I didn't want a priest, but he came anyway. Anna told him no and to come another day.

He said that woman, and he meant me, that woman is an Italian mother, so she is a Catholic and must hear what I have to tell her. I bring the word of God.

Can you imagine? He practically pushed Anna away in order to get by her. She shook her head at this and left. I don't know what else she could have done. Or me. I was weak and in no condition to get out of the bed and chase him away.

This priest, not from my mother's church, told me when I got home I had to let 'God' decide what was best. I didn't know what he was talking about. Then he said, you must use no methods to stop babies from coming, not rhythm or anything else.

He said you must let your husband stay inside you until he is finished.

Can you imagine a priest, who isn't supposed to do or think of such things, can you imagine him telling me this, a young girl, not yet twenty? I was furious. I told him to mind his own business. And then I said if my husband was home, we would make love as often and as much and how we liked, and he and God would have nothing to do with it. I screamed this at him.

He made the sign of the cross and left as fast as he could, a young Irishman. Not much older than I was, but you should have seen him then, bent over his rosary beads like an old man. Anna came back immediately and said she was so sorry. I told her it wasn't her fault. What else could I say?

Finally, after many days, I don't remember how many, Mamma and Cino came to take me home. Oh how happy I was to hug and kiss Aldo and Nino, but I missed the sweet nurses and Anna. They were lovely, young, and so good. I never forgot their kindness.

Mamma found the cradle in the basement and cleaned it up while I was away. She waited to get things ready for the baby. She wouldn't do it until she knew the baby was born and healthy. Bad luck, she said, to do it too early. She and Charles took the cradle upstairs and put it next to my bed. Mamma and Aunt Abelia got some new blankets, pretty and fresh, from a woman at their church. Beautiful new things for this beautiful bambina in our lives. Bellissima bambina. I started calling her Bella. She had a round soft face with deep, dark eyes, like her papà. She latched onto me and drank her milk, her little fingers around one of mine. It was nice for a time to have some happiness. But it didn't last.

Cino brought the news. The appeal was denied. All I knew was I had to see Ermo.

15
ALL REMEDIES EXHAUSTED

Wethersfield, Connecticut
June 1919

E rasmo could do nothing. A mouse in a trap cannot do anything. Lia had their baby. Cino told him. A baby girl, Amalia. Lia calls her Bella. She is una bella bambina. But this news broke Erasmo. He was not there when his bella figlia was born. He could not hold her in his arms or comfort his brave Lia. He was sure Giù heard his despair through the wall between their cells.

Giù called out to him. It will be okay, brother, he said. You will soon be home.

Erasmo wanted to believe this.

It was March now. Both Giù and Erasmo waited for news from Noble Pierce and Patrick McDonaugh. On the day they arrived, Erasmo thought they would not come. It was a day of high winds and heavy rain, dark as night. But the guards said their lawyers were waiting to see them. This means good news,

Erasmo thought. Who would come out on such a day to deliver news no one wanted to hear, or to give?

The brothers, in shackles, were brought to a small, windowless meeting room furnished with a long wooden table and four chairs, two on each side. Erasmo and Giuseppe sat on one side. Noble Pierce and Patrick McDonough on the other. The lawyers said hello and put out their hands to shake the hands in handcuffs on the other side of the table. But they would not look the brothers in the eye. Erasmo felt bile rise in his throat, his heart starting to pump. He knew what they would say.

It was true, the appeal had been denied. Giù let out a moan, but Erasmo asked what is next. He did not know what to expect, but he thought there must be a next step.

There was still time, Noble Pierce said. We filed a petition to be heard by the state Board of Pardons. This would be heard on the ninth of June.

Erasmo wasn't sure what that meant. His only question, What is the new date?

Noble Pierce told him the execution was set for June twenty-seventh. But don't think about that, he said. There is still time. This petition to the board, these men can change the sentence. Not a pardon; that is unlikely, but a change in sentence to life in prison. At least there would be time to prepare for a new trial, to overturn the verdict.

Giù put his head in his shackled hands. What's the use? he said. I would rather die than spend my life here. Just let me die, Mr. Noble Pierce.

Erasmo put his hand on his brother's back. No, Giù. This is not the time to give up. We've waited this long. We can wait more.

But back in his cell, Erasmo sat on his cot and moaned quietly into his hands. He had many thoughts he kept to himself. There is nothing I can do. I cannot save us. I don't know what is left for us to hope for. This board of men who have power to save us, why should I believe they will be any different from the men in the court who told lies or the men on the jury who listened to lies and did nothing? This country does not want us and will kill us to be rid of us. He lay down and turned to the wall, despairing silently, so Giù wouldn't hear.

In April, Erasmo worried. Why hasn't Lia been here? Why doesn't Cino bring her to me? When will I see my children, my daughter, two months old already? In these dark days in a cell that gave no sign of spring, Erasmo's fears were wide-ranging. He even began to doubt his Lia. Was she waiting for him? How hard this time must be for her. Maybe too hard. Maybe she cannot bear it. He began to suspect Cino. His cousin's visits were less frequent. But when he came, he spoke of how hard he was working for their freedom. These words made it impossible for Erasmo to feed his doubts. He needed Cino. Even if Giù had given up, Erasmo had not.

And then a miracle. One morning a hazy ray of sunlight shone through his barred window. A guard jangled his keys and told Erasmo to get up from his cot. He had visitors. Lawyers? asked Erasmo. No lawyers, he was told. The guard put on the shackles and let him to the meeting room.

What about Giù? Erasmo asked.

The guard said no, just you.

When the guard opened the door to the room, Erasmo saw Cino, who took Erasmo's hands in his briefly but then walked past him. Erasmo turned to see where he was going, wondering why he had left in such a hurry. When he turned back to enter the room, he saw them. Lia. In her arms, Bella.

You have twenty minutes alone, the guard said before he walked out and closed the door.

Before he could go to them, Erasmo had to lean on the

table. His legs were weakening. Lia rushed to him. She was holding Bella, but he could only see her dark hair and eyes peering out from Lia's coat where she had kept Bella for warmth in this cold place. Lia pulled her out so her father could see his beautiful daughter, and then Lia embraced her Ermo. With her free hand, she pulled him to her, whispering his name again and again in his ear.

This was a balm. It was true. Of his many doubts, he doubted his own name. Who was he anymore? Was he a man, a man of property, a man with his own business, home, and family? Who was he? For so long now it seemed, he was no more than the rat who scurried in his cell. But here was proof of the man he was. A husband. A father.

The family of three stood there, together, for some time, crying into each other, Bella softly, Erasmo and Lia, stifling sobs. Oranges, Erasmo thought. In their circle was the scent of oranges. Like home.

When Erasmo was steady, they sat in the two chairs on one side of the wooden table in the meeting room. Erasmo held his daughter between his cuffed hands. He looked into her deep brown eyes, felt her soft, full cheeks, rosy. She was well, a healthy beauty. And she knew he was her father. He saw it in her. He was sure of it.

The husband and wife talked. Erasmo was full of questions, how was she getting along, was she eating? She looked pale and thin. Too thin. The boys—how were Aldo and Nino?

She assured him she was well, and the boys. Her mother and Zia Abelia were taking good care of them and they had money. He was too weary to ask too much. It would be too much to hear about the money, the donations, the loans he knew must be sustaining them. He was supposed to be providing, not relatives and strangers. But there was only so much he could think about. No, in the minutes remaining he would be quiet. He wanted only this, his Lia and his Bella. Now he would have a picture in his brain to think about again and again back in his cell.

* * *

On the ninth of June the brothers learned that the Board of Pardons would not change the sentence. No pardon, not even to life in prison. Now Erasmo knew nothing awaited them but death. He lashed out at Noble Pierce, who visited him in his cell, when he read to him the words of the prosecuting attorney, the same lying man, Hugh Alcorn.

This man who wanted them dead told the board, who had the power to change the sentence, something that surely must have damned the brothers, taking away any chance of freedom. It was a truth, what he said, but it was not justification for hanging two brothers. 'They are anarchists,' he told the board. 'And for this reason, it doesn't matter if they are guilty of murder.'

How can this be? Erasmo asked of Noble Pierce. Are we to be hanged because of what we believe? Are anarchists now to be hanged? Then where are these guilty anarchists sentenced to be hanged? There are none here in this jail, and yet are there not many in the state of Connecticut alone? Why are we to die for our beliefs?

Erasmo was at that moment quite beside himself.

Get us a new trial or leave us alone, he said to Noble Pierce. You are part of this injustice if you can do no more to help us.

Once alone in his cell on that day, rocking back and forth on the edge of his cot, Erasmo continued to ask, Is there nothing to be done? But knowing there was nothing.

On June tenth, two new men came to see the shackled brothers who sat at the wooden table in the meeting room.

There would be no more visits from Noble Pierce or Patrick McDonough, who sent word with these two new lawyers that they had done all they could. Now a Judge, Joseph Tuttle, and a Mr. Salvator D'Esopo would do everything in their power, they said, to help the brothers against the counting down of the clock.

In a few days we will file a motion for a new trial, based on new evidence, the judge who was a lawyer said.

Giù barely looked up at this news. Erasmo knew he had given up, but he wouldn't say such a thing to his brother. Erasmo would despair but could not give up. His mind was full of Lia and his sons and Bella. He returned to the picture of her in his mind, her head of dark hair, like her mother's, deep brown eyes, like his, and rosy cheeks.

Erasmo looked at Judge Tuttle and the lawyer Mr. D'Esopo. The judge was like all the others, pale, tired and grey. But this Salvator D'Esopo had fire in him, young and full of confidence. Pieno di sé, in truth, puffed up like a rooster, so full of himself. Erasmo made note of his trimmed fingernails, fine shirt, cufflinks, and suit. He reminded Erasmo of the officials from Rome who sometimes came to Saviano to meet with the important men at the municipio. Erasmo never trusted any of them. And he didn't trust this Salvator D'Esopo. He didn't have time for a preening man. There was too little time left.

The next day, Cino came to meet with Erasmo. Giù wouldn't leave his cell. He was sick, he said. And Erasmo knew the sickness that was in his lungs was more in his heart. Cino sat down at the table and said yes, it was true. Salvator D'Esopo was their new lawyer and a very successful paisano.

You're kidding me, said Erasmo. That man is no paisano.

Cino had to admit, the D'Esopo's family came from the north. His father, his brother, and he were prominenti. They are among the rich in Hartford. Educated at Yale. Ivy league, very important college, very expensive. They have influence, Cino said.

Erasmo wanted to know why this important strutting rooster wanted to represent the shoemaker from Saviano and his brother. Cino said it was the court's decision. Don't worry, he said. It's paid for. We have a fund for your defense.

Erasmo had to thank his cousin. He had to appreciate all Cino was doing for him and his family, but he didn't have to trust the rooster.

That night the guard who brought their tins of food said to Erasmo, you must have connections. The Italian you have now, him and his brother Ferdinand, they speak to your kind all over the state. They want to make you people more like Americans, not so foreign. These brothers are friends with the governor, and they don't trust immigrants any more than he does. The guard sucked his teeth and looked at Erasmo with narrowed eyes when he said this. He was near insult and Erasmo felt his chest begin to heave. So you must have friends in high places, the guard said, putting the tin through the door, waiting for Erasmo to take it.

Erasmo didn't move. He did not like the sound of this.

Take it or you won't eat, said the guard. No skin off my nose.

Erasmo took the tin and said nothing, but when the guard turned to leave, he said, My brother and I don't need that kind of help. The guard shrugged and walked to Giù's cell.

Erasmo had to think about it, what the guard said. He had to think about two Italian brothers who were friends with the governor, who were well educated and rich. What makes them so different from us, two Italian brothers who worked hard to have a place in America? It was a puzzle. But Erasmo knew the answer. Injustice.

* * *

Erasmo has no patience. There is no clock in his cell, but he hears one ticking.

Things are happening over which he has no control. He knows his fate is in the hands of others. He paces back and forth with this knowledge. On the twelfth of June, the preening rooster and the other one, Judge Tuttle, did indeed file a motion for a new trial in Superior Court based on new evidence. That afternoon they come again to meet with the brothers to explain the motion.

Although Giù is already detached, accepting that he will die, Erasmo is not and wants to hear.

The new evidence, the Italian says, is from something that he has learned by following leads. He has found two new witnesses who are willing to say in court that on the night of the murder they saw two men not resembling Erasmo or Joseph heading south, away from the scene of the murder.

Giù is not listening, but Erasmo is and interrupts. This is what others have said already, what Charles Pierce said in the courtroom, the woman, and others. What difference does this make? he asks.

It is true, the lawyer says, others have already testified to seeing two men who were not you and your brother. But these new witnesses will say in a new trial something more, something important, that the two unknown men they saw that night were moving very quickly, they were running, to a car waiting for them, with the engine going, and that these two men got into that waiting car with the engine going and sped away.

This gets Erasmo's attention. He is not a lawyer, but he sees that this is new evidence. He and Giù were framed, he thinks. Two men killed Frank Palmese and made a getaway. He knows enough about crime in America to know that bad men moved quickly in getaway cars. He has heard that it is just like that in the movies. A friend of Cino's who knew English went to see some cousins in Bridgeport. There this friend had seen moving images in a theatre. The pictures were of cars and shootouts with the police. Erasmo could see it in his imagination. The difference was the crime in the movie was a bank robbery, not a murder. He wonders now if this Italian lawyer might be able to help. Judge Tuttle says nothing. Giù is not paying attention. Erasmo has hope.

In the days following, Erasmo is waiting and pacing. A man in a cell, an animal in a cage.

*　*　*

The clock that is not there but is heard just the same, ticks. And yet there has been no word. It is now June twenty-fifth. Erasmo is frantic. He has been abandoned. Where is Lia? Where are his sons, his daughter? Has the Italian given up on them, too? Will no new last minute lawyer come?

Late in the afternoon, He receives word. Mr. Salvator D'Esopo, without the other one, the judge, has come to meet with Erasmo and Giuseppe. They are bound, hands and feet and led to the dark room. They sit and face the Italian.

Judge Tuttle has quit the case, he says. I have come alone to tell you what has happened with your case. And so he begins.

On the sixteenth of June, I met with Superior Court Justice, Lucien Burpee, D'Esopo says.

Erasmo knows this name. This Lucien Burpee is another of the old men. His only passion in the courtroom was to sentence the brothers to death. He relished the words, hanged by the neck until dead. He has no use for Erasmo and his brother. He only wants to see them dead.

Is he the one in charge of a new trial? Erasmo asks.

The answer is yes. Erasmo thinks this is not good. And Erasmo is right. Judge Burpee has issued a demurrer. When the Italian says this, the brothers look at each other and then at the Italian.

A denial, the lawyer says. It means the petition for a new trial has been denied. He pauses to see their response. Erasmo and Giù are quiet. The Italian continues. The new evidence changes nothing, the Judge decided.

But what about these other men, the two new witnesses, the getaway car? Erasmo asks.

The Italian only shakes his head.

This is more than Erasmo can bear. He wants Giù to have patience, hope, but how can he help him when Erasmo himself is nearing the end of hope? He sees Lia, his sons and his daughter in his head. Lia and the babies won't let him be.

It that all? he asks. What remains to be done?

There is more. On the nineteenth of June, the Italian lawyer had an audience with Governor Holcomb. He claims the governor had the power to call the Board of Pardons into special session to reconsider the brothers' case.

Once again Erasmo feels a rush of blood in his veins. It is something. The governor, he is powerful, but why is the Italian looking down when he says this.

Governor Holcomb refused to call a special session, the Italian says. What's more, he declines to intercede.

What does this mean? Erasmo demands. You are Italian. Tell me in a language I can understand. The Italian continues. Now Erasmo understands the words, but he finds none to comfort him.

On the twenty-first of June, D'Esopo arranged for the Royal Italian Government, through its Consul General of Italy in New York, to make a request that Governor Holcomb intercede on behalf of the condemned men. The Italian explains this and reads the correspondence to the condemned men. On the twenty-fifth of June, at 12:30 p.m., the Royal Consular Agent of Italy sent a telegram to Governor Holcomb marked 'extra rush.'

'To His Excellency Marcus Holcomb,' it began. 'Regarding the midnight capital punishment of two Italian subjects, the Perretta brothers, as the lawyers for the convicted believe that there is new evidence to be discovered, I beg your excellency to grant to the condemned a reprieve in order that a further investigation might be made.' Signed, The Consul General of Italy.

The Italian takes a sip of water from a cup on the table. He reads Holcomb's reply: 'The Perretta brothers have had recourse to every available tribunal in Connecticut, including an application for a new trial for alleged newly discovered evidence, which was refused by the court. I must decline to intervene further in this case.' Marcus H. Holcomb, Governor.

Governor Holcomb would not intercede, D'Esopo says. Even Amalia went to see him, the Italian adds.

This captures Erasmo's attention. Lia went to see the governor? Erasmo asks.

The Italian tells him she went with all three babies. She implored him to have mercy, but he would not be moved.

Erasmo can see her, Nino and Bella in her arms, Aldo hanging onto her skirt. How hard that was for her, to go there, to the governor, a man who would represent everything she despised, for her to go there, to humble herself in that way. He knows now that she would do anything to save him. But even this, a mother soon to be a widow, three babies soon to be fatherless, if even this would not make a difference, what hope can there be? A chill runs through him.

The Italian is nervous. Erasmo knows. He must tell the brothers that he has exhausted all legal remedies. There is nothing more that can be done. Judge Tuttle has abandoned the case. And so must he.

Giù sits unmoved, his eyes vacant. Erasmo is stunned into silence. He feels fear leave his body, from his head through to his fingertips. His heart is beating as if he had just settled down for a rest. His breath is rhythmic. He is calm and doesn't understand how this can be. It is as though he has been under the sea for so long all struggling has passed.

He calls Salvator D'Esopo, paisano. Grazie, he says, molte grazie.

They are quiet for a time. When the guard comes to take the brothers back to their cells, the lawyer instructs the guard to take off the handcuffs.

The guard says he cannot.

The lawyer says these men are still bound at the feet. They present no danger. I want to shake hands with these men before I leave. Must I call the warden? he demands more than asks.

The guard complies. He will remove the handcuffs, allowing time for the men to clasp hands.

First, Giù, who takes Salvator's hand, looks at the man who devoted many hours to their cause, and says grazie. He withdraws his hands and points them in the direction of the guard, who cuffs him again. Giù sits down and lowers his head, shoulders rolled. He looks like a man already gone.

The guard says of Erasmo, this man I don't trust. I will remove his handcuffs, but I am drawing my gun, he says, looking at Erasmo.

Erasmo takes Salvator's hands in his. You alone have defended us, he says. You are the only one who looked at us as human, who fought for us. For this I am thankful. He grips the lawyer's hands hard. But my Lia and bambini, what is to be done? I must find some answer.

Salvator D'Esopo says nothing. The reply with no words is clear. There is nothing more to be done.

Erasmo, back in his cell, loses the resignation that was briefly his. Again, he rocks. I lose my brain, he says, I lose my brain. He can think of nothing that will help his cause, save his brother's life, save his.

That night, he is restless. He is cold one minute, sweating the next. It is as if the nfruenza has returned. He cannot control his shaking. He cannot think clearly. And then the calm returns. He breathes deeply and stops shaking. He is able finally to think, and he thinks of only one person, the governor. He is a puzzle, this man who cannot be moved, not by the Italian's many attempts, not by Lia, this beautiful Madonna with her babies. Nothing has moved him to intercede to save the brothers. If I could talk to him, Erasmo thinks, but that is impossible. If I could tell him our story, the truth about all the lies he has heard, surely an honest man, a decent man would see, would understand the injustice that has been done.

Erasmo once again has resolve. He calls for the guard. With urgency, he calls.

Giù calls to his brother from the next cell. Brother, he asks, what is it? Are you all right?

Erasmo assures, yes, he is all right. I have one more thing I must do, he says. But Giù does not respond. Erasmo knows his brother is done with ideas and only wants it over with. But he has one thing he must do. Finally, the guard comes.

You are making quite a racket, he says.

But he listens as Erasmo tells what he wants, tells the guard it is his right. And it is. He has learned this from the lawyers. All of them have told him he has this right.

Soon the guard brings him a piece of paper, a pen, and an inkwell. I will need more than one piece of paper, Erasmo says. I will need many pages. The guard makes a groaning noise, but he goes for more paper. Erasmo is exercising his right, and the guard must comply. He returns with more paper.

Erasmo prepares for his task: to write a letter to Governor Marcus H. Holcomb. He sits down at the small wooden table pushed up against the back wall of his cell. A bare electric bulb screwed into the socket in the ceiling dimly lights the room. In twenty-four hours, Erasmo and Giuseppe will climb the scaffold to the hanging machine in the Wethersfield prison. The guard who brings the brothers the watery soup in the tins has told Erasmo about the device made to jerk a man into the air by the neck.

Quite a machine, that one. Makes a man die fast. You'll be glad of it, too, the guard said. He looked at Erasmo, when he said it, to see his reaction. Erasmo had to look away. He didn't want the guard to see him shake at the news of the hanging machine.

Now again he is struggling to overcome his fear. Now is the time to be calm. He must focus on the task at hand.

A stack of prison paper sits before him on the desk. There are very specific rules about its use at the top of the first page. *Write only on Ruled Lines. The inmate must confine himself to family or business of his own.* Erasmo knows he will write many pages. There is so much to be said, so many injustices, so many things presented incorrectly. He must make the governor understand. This letter is his last chance to be heard.

He smooths the writing paper against the rough surface of the desk and picks up the fountain pen the guard has given him. He carefully dips it into the inkwell. Using his fingernail to pull the lever away from the barrel, Erasmo watches the bubbles foam as the black ink is absorbed into the two little holes in the nib.

The guard watches to be certain the pen does not become a weapon. Erasmo thinks, let this pen be my sword. His heart is beating fast. If Governor Holcomb is an honorable man, he will see, by this letter, that two brothers have been falsely accused.

Erasmo writes tentatively, he wants no mistakes. The pen makes its first marks, a number one with a raised, small zero next to it, underlined twice in the middle of the first line. Erasmo pauses. This first mark is good, written in a steady hand. He is not an educated man, his English is not good, but he can write in Italian, and he knows the writing must be clean and neat. Erasmo must use proper language; he cannot use the dialect of his village. The interpreter who will prepare the letter in English for His Excellency must see that Erasmo is not a peasant, but a man with a trade, a shoemaker, with a home and a business of his own, with a wife and three babies. Erasmo and his brother are not murderers. Erasmo must make the interpreter, the Honorable Governor Holcomb, and anyone who will read this letter, see the brothers' innocence.

His Excellency, Governor Holcomb:

I have decided to write this fateful letter regarding our unexpected, cruel sentence inflicted upon us, the innocent. Excellency, Governor, if what we write does not seem true, it is because they have made you understand that we are very murderous. We assure you we are two innocent men and that our death sentence is based on all lies inflicted upon us. We were in bed when this happened. Excellency, Governor Holcomb. Don't give your permission to make us two innocent victims. Be brave. Do everything you can to give us a new process, without injustice.

Excellency, Governor Holcomb, make an investigation and you will find that Frank Palmese, the victim, did not say 'Erasmo shot me and Giuseppe cut me.' There were two nurses present who can tell you the truth.

Excellency, Governor Holcomb, on the morning of June 3, 1918, my house was surrounded and the officers who entered declared that I was under arrest, demanding if I knew anything about their questions, but I knew nothing of their questions because a man who sleeps knows nothing of what happens in the streets. Then my brother and I were handcuffed and taken to the hospital.

The injured man was lying on the bed, and he supposedly gets Erasmo by the arm and says, 'He shot me and Giuseppe cut me.' This is not true.

Excellency, Governor Holcomb, the interpreter asked him if he knew us, and Frank Palmese responded yes. And the interpreter asked him again if he had any quarrel with us, and Palmese said no.

Who will protect us from these lies?

Also, I have seen in the court, policemen who were never in my house before, and yet they were on the stand testifying as if they had been there. And yet, the one officer who was at my house, who knew us, Officer Dolan, was not in court. Why wasn't he allowed to testify? Because he would have told the truth, that he was the only one on night duty, on the beat, and at my house that night, and with his own mouth told me, 'Don't worry, from 10:30 p.m. tonight, I have not seen you in the street.' And this is all true, because anyone can tell you Officer Dolan was on the beat that night, and he can tell you what I am saying now.

This shows we were all framed up.

Excellency, Governor Holcomb, I again beg you; use all your influence; don't let two brothers die so cruelly. Someday, Excellency, Governor Holcomb, our innocence will be discovered and made known. Then it will be too late.

You will know all if you investigate.

His letter goes on for many pages. Erasmo knows what he wants to say, that the judicial system is determined against him and his brother and has been from the start. He looks over what he has written. Surely I have made a good case, he thinks.

He ends his letter,

Final regards from the brothers Perretta.

His only hope now is that the governor is an honorable man.

162

16

THE STRAIGHT WAY LOST

New Britain, Connecticut
August 3, 1995

W e wanted to change the world. We were young. We
thought it was possible. Or maybe Ermo never
believed it, really. Maybe all that he did was for me. Even
today, this is hard to say, to think about.

In those days, though, our gruppo, was willing to endure
anything for our beliefs. We knew that injustice could be made
right. It was in us to do it. We might have to burn the corruption out, but in the ashes . . . you know that story of what comes
from ashes. We believed it. It wasn't just a story to us. But in
the months when we waited with hope sometimes and then
with despair, I forgot about the days of the gruppo. I only
wanted Ermo back. Both of them, Ermo and Giù, I wanted
them home.

I was not well, but because of my mother and my aunt, I
lived. They made me eat, they took care of the boys, and my

milk did not dry up, even though I was skin and bone. I was withering away because I couldn't see Ermo. The more they kept me away, the worse I became. I begged Cino, but he said no. I knew he thought I couldn't take the prison, but I could endure for one hour what Ermo had to endure every day. Still, he would not take me, and my mother wouldn't hear of it, not until the day I passed out and would not wake up. That was the day my milk stopped coming. They sent for the doctor, but I was conscious then and said I wouldn't see him. I told my mother not to let him in. I was out of my mind. If I can't take Bella to see Ermo, then let us die. That is when Cino said he would take me, but I had to see the doctor first.

It took time for me to recover. And time for Ermo and Giù was running out. Mamma said I must gain weight.

Do you want Erasmo to see a scarecrow? You must eat, she told me.

And I did. I ate the creamy pasta. I ate Zia Abelia's cake. My milk came and soon I would see Ermo.

I remember it well. It was a sunny day near the end of April. It was Pasquetta. I know, because Mamma and Zietta were complaining in the kitchen that they didn't have every-thing needed for pastiera and were trying to make substitutions. We were consumed with the reality of time, trying to put it out of our minds. But Mamma and Zietta wanted the boys to know some joy, so they dyed eggs for them and made Easter bread. They wanted to make the pastiera for Ermo and Giù, but I refused to take it.

I will make my own bread for them, I told Mamma. Not for Easter. I will bring plain bread with butter.

So they made the pastiera for Cino and one for the priest. I said nothing more.

On that morning, I didn't want to think about the date we all feared, knowing that nothing good was happening with the lawyers. I, too, wanted some happiness. I tried to think of good things. I would be taking Bella to see her father for the first time. That thought gave me courage for the visit. I washed in scented water, using a few drops of the orange oil Aunt Abelia had brought from Saviano, only to be used on special occasions. The last time I washed in it was the day of our wedding. While I dressed, I even hummed a song I knew as a little girl. *Lo tujo mme daje e lu mio tiene.* Ha! I still remember. It is in dialect. *Still keep my heart, and give me, give me thine.* So lovely.

Even though it was still a little cold, I wore a dress I knew Ermo liked, a soft fabric with flowers, but I had to wear a coat over it for the car ride to the prison. When Cino came, Bella and I were ready. Mamma and Aunt Abelia fussed over us.

Are you dressed warmly enough? Let us wrap Bella in another blanket. Aunt Abelia said and brought me one of the blankets she had bought from the woman at the church when Bella was born.

The boys were up, sitting at the table eating Easter bread and rolling their dyed eggs to the edge and back. Before I left, Aldo came to me and said he wanted me to take something to Papà for him. It was a pencil drawing he had made, shapes of lines and circles, nothing real, but he said it was us, Mamma and Papà, Aldo, Nino, and Bella.

See us? He asked, looking up at me. Tell Papà to come home.

It was the first time I realized he knew his father was gone. I bent down to take his drawing.

I will give it to Papà, I said.

I hugged my son for his thoughtfulness. On the drive to the prison, I opened my bag to see Aldo's folded drawing next to Ermo's gift to me, the yellow handkerchief with the beautiful lace trim. I pulled it out to wipe my eyes. The new flowers along the side of the road made me sad.

Inside the prison there was no more spring. How could anyone live in such a place? You could feel death there. I held Bella close to me but had to give her to Cino while I was searched. After, I was thankful that I could keep my coat for the visit and put Bella inside, against my chest to keep her warm. Cino and I were led to a dark room to wait for Ermo.

I would not be seeing 'Joseph.' that is what the guard called Giù. The guard told me, only his brother, Erasmo. A wife and child could see a father. That was all.

When they brought Ermo in, Cino left us. What is there to say? I will never forget the look on his face when he saw Bella peeking out from my coat. His daughter. I held him with her between us, and we cried. We sat down at the table and Ermo held Bella in his two cuffed hands. She stared into his eyes. He said she recognized him. I'm sure that was true.

I asked if he was okay. He looked so thin and pale. He only shrugged. What more could he say? Things in his miserable prison would not change. He was well, but he continued to worry about Giù. I knew he didn't want to worry me anymore, so he asked many questions about us.

We are all well, I told him. Mamma and Zietta see to it. Nothing to worry about. I didn't tell him I closed the shop or about our money troubles. And he didn't ask. I don't think he could stand to know.

He continued to look down at Bella. A daughter, he said, after two healthy sons.

It was something to be thankful for in those terrible times, but how could we be thankful? Our world was closing in on us. There was no future, and we didn't talk of one, not after Ermo only shook his head when I asked him if there was any news from the lawyers.

I gave Ermo Aldo's drawing and told him what his son had said. I wanted to make Ermo happy, if only for a little while, but it didn't work. The drawing only made him sadder, knowing he was not around to be a father to his sons and to Bella. After that, we hardly talked. We stayed quiet to make time go slowly. We stayed that way until the guard told me it was time to go. How can I tell you how hard that parting was? He held onto Bella as though she might break if he let her go, pulling her to his chest. When he gave her to me, he held onto my arms until I felt them bruise. We didn't know when we would see each other again, and in our minds was the fear that the next time would be the last.

* * *

No one was saving Ermo and Giù. The Italian government was writing to Governor Holcomb to pardon the brothers. The governor did nothing. There was no more to be done, even Cino said it, but I couldn't accept that. I was frantic, my hair was falling out. On the day before the governor was going to let them die, I gathered up the children, got on the train to Hartford, and went to see this Marcus Holcomb. Don't ask me how I got there. I see everything through tears and anger. I walked up the stairs of the capital building and was stopped at the door by two policemen who told me I couldn't come in without a letter of invitation. A letter of invitation. I had to laugh. I told them I had no letter, but that I wouldn't leave. The children were crying. There were so many people waiting behind us. They heard every word. Some said let her in. They were taking my side.

Someone came then and escorted me to the governor's office. I waited outside the door, the children crying still. We waited a long time. Finally, a large woman with grey hair piled on top her head opened the door. I stood to go in, but she stood in my way and took off her glasses, letting them hang from a long chain around her neck. I remember this because I thought she was getting ready to hit me. In a harsh voice, she told me the governor could not see me. She told me to come back tomorrow. That is too late, I screamed at her. She was trying to close the door, but I wouldn't let her. Soon the two policemen from the entrance came.

I began to walk away, screaming at all of them. 'Morite. Brucerete all'inferno, tutti. Vi maledico,' I cursed at them. I was out of my mind. I knew he was in there. I know he heard me.

Sconvolta, yes, that's it. I was distraught. I don't know how we got home. When I left that morning, I was a sane woman. When I returned that night, I was someone else. My mother took the children from me. My aunt took me to wash and put me to bed. She closed the door.

I heard the doorbell chime from the street. I heard my mother and Aunt Abelia letting people in and coming up the stairs. I didn't get up to see, but I heard voices. I know I heard Jennifer and Charles Pierce and Cino.

They let me be. The next morning I would go to the prison again, with the children, to say goodbye.

I woke up early and opened the door. Francesco was there and Marianne. They had their two children with them, Michele and Antonio. You know them, your grandfather and grandmother, your uncle and your father, little Michele. They had come the night before, when I heard the doorbell chiming.

My mother and aunt washed and dressed me, I was not myself, and then they dressed the children. Before we left with Cino for the prison, Francesco gave me a letter for the brothers. It was from Nicoletta, their mother. He wanted them to have it before he got there. He was to see them later in the afternoon.

My mind is so full now. You understand if I don't say anything more. I need to be alone with my thoughts.

17

NO GREATER SORROW

Wethersfield, Connecticut
June, 1919

A malia is in the prison in the cell with Erasmo. She has just come from saying goodbye to Giù, who held her hand and touched Bella's head. He was calm and told her not to worry, only to pray for them. Amalia did not tell him she had no prayers to give.

There is nothing that hurt Amalia and Erasmo more than these moments. They share their thoughts, thinking the same things. They were so young and yet now so old. How could it be that we were just children only a few years ago? She pictures him in his shop the first time she saw him. He remembers her at the Sanchini's when he knew he would marry her. He holds the babies. They don't know what is happening, but they are happy to be with their papà. Amalia gives him his mother's letter. He puts in on the cot. He will read it later and make sure Giù gets it, too. They talk to Giù through the wall. Lia cannot understand what he is saying.

Erasmo tells her Giù is praying. He sees the priest every day. It comforts him, he says.

That is good, they agree, but Erasmo says no prayers and sees no priest. There is no comfort for him.

The guard comes to tell Amalia she must go. Erasmo holds her, Bella in her arms, the boys by their parents' sides. She doesn't move to leave. Another guard comes to take her away.

Erasmo, says no, leave her.

Think of your children, one guard says.

Amalia cannot stop herself, she laughs, her face red and streaked with tears. How can you say such a thing to us? Does anyone care about these children? The lawyers, the judge, the governor? No one. Shut your mouth and be ashamed, she screams at them.

One of the guards holds Erasmo, the other takes Amalia by the arm. The children are crying.

One minute more, she begs. Let me go, for just one moment. She rushes back to her husband. They embrace. She puts her hands on his head and runs her fingers through his hair. Amore mio, marito mio, she whispers to him.

He cries into her neck, the scent again of oranges. She is pulled from him. They both know this is the moment of greatest dread. He hears her screams in the corridor.

A curse most dreadful. Una maledizione on everyone who is taking him from us, she screams.

Erasmo collapses on his cot. I lose my brain, he says again and again.

By afternoon when Francesco comes to say goodbye, Erasmo is in a state of delirium. He will not see his brother.

Francesco goes to Giù, who says he is at peace and blames no one. He tells his brother non disperare.

Francesco says there may yet be a midnight reprieve.

Giù only shakes his head. He gives his brother the letter

from their mother. Give it to Lia, he says. She will want to keep it. Pray with me, Ciccio, Giù says to his brother.

The two stay together until the guard comes. Francesco tries again to see Erasmo, but he is not able to rise from his stupor.

Outside the prison walls, Francesco opens his mother's letter. He reads.

Miei cari figli,

How I love you, my boys, how I miss you. I long for you to come home. Your papà and I are growing old. We need you here, to help us with the oranges and the lemons. The trees are too many and too difficult for me alone, now that Papà hardly works. Who will help me with the customers in the bar? And more, how can we help you, so far away?

She continues. *But don't despair. You must trust in God to bring you back to us. Don't lose hope. I won't stop praying for you.*

After reading this much, Francesco wonders if he should give the letter back to Lia. When she gave it to him, she said she didn't have the strength to read it. Then he reads the end.

Why did you ever go to that place? Come home.

This is more than Francesco can bear. He will tell Amalia about the letter, but he will not give it to her. He crumbles it up and lets the wind take it. He leaves to be with the women and children who wait for him on Cherry Street.

The hours pass. The brothers are led from their cells. There will be no midnight reprieve.

They mount the stairs to the noose. Weak and trembling, both, they must be helped. Giuseppe will be first. Erasmo is glad. He doesn't want his brother to witness his death. Better to be first, to get it over, he thinks.

Giuseppe is joined by two priests, one on each side. One holds a crucifix to his lips, which he kisses again and again. Erasmo turns his head away. Then he closes his eyes and will not open them again until it is done. He imagines a large eagle flying above him. Even in this dark place, even with his eyes shut, Erasmo sees the shadow above his head. The sounds, he does not want to hear. He cannot stop the bird's final cry. He remembers the birds in the hills outside of Saviano. He and his brothers used to hunt birds there. Little ones, songbirds. Holding one dead in his hand the first time made Erasmo sad, so lovely, the song so sweet. Someone touches him. He is awakened from his thoughts of the birds.

Erasmo looks down to see he is wearing a brown suit and a striped shirt. He remembers being helped to get dressed. There is a white collar, around which is a black bow tie. He thinks of his brother, also in a suit, his black. Now he remembers where he is. Yes, the suits. These were from the prison, probably worn by other men on this same scaffold. He wonders why the people in this country think it is important to wear a suit to be hanged. An odd thought to have at this moment. His stomach lurches when the priests walk toward him.

No, he says. Don't come to me.

You want the crucifix? they ask.

He tries to wave them away but remembers his hands are bound. He only shakes his head.

Lasciatemi. Leave me, he says to them before the black hood is lowered over his head. He pays no attention to the priests but can hear them praying. He is preoccupied with these last seconds of his life, panting into the darkness, barely able to stand, as scared as a wounded animal. The priests have come to stand by him regardless of his rejection. Their prayers, now mere mumbling, his blood pounding in his head.

Suddenly all is quiet. Calma. He feels the strange calm again, just as he had when the Italian lawyer said there was nothing more to be done, and Erasmo had thanked him for trying to save him and his brother.

The rope is adjusted around Erasmo's neck. He should have read his mother's letter, he thinks. He wishes he had not tossed it aside only to have the guard give it to Giù before he could read it.

Mamma, he thinks. He is in her garden at home. She is serving wine to Papà. His brothers are there, rifles slung over their shoulders. Back from the hills, they have songbirds in their pouches. The family will feast on the succulent tiny creatures tonight. He hears laughter and sees his children, Aldo, Nino, and Bella, playing among the oranges. He almost has to close his eyes to sudden glare, but then he sees her. Lia, the sun framing her face. What a smile she has. He remembers all the days when her smile intoxicated him. Erasmo feels a sudden pull and is released into the air. He soars, then a crack—like thunder—and he flies to her.

18

REVELATIONS

New Britain, Connecticut
August 10, 1995

There is more to explain but little left to say. Why? Because what I learned and when I learned it, time had run out. And nothing I learned could have changed anything, anyway.

After I lost my Ermo, I also lost my mind. Nothing that had come before was as bad as that time. You cannot imagine the pain that comes with the details of such a death. The day they were gone, we were told to come for the bodies. My mother told me the priest would bury Giù in the churchyard, but not Ermo. Of course, that would be so. Everyone knew Giù was no anarchist. He prayed with the priests, he confessed his sins to them. What sins? Little ones, venial sins only, I am sure, because that is all he had to confess.

But not Ermo, according to the priest, Ermo was a true sinner. He was not married in the church. He did not believe in God. He was an anarchist. These were the things that vile 'man of God,' was telling me through my mother. When she said these things, I tore my hair and scratched my face with anger. I screamed at Mamma to never take another dime from that church. Ermo died by his beliefs, I told her. A dying man will kiss the hand of a priest, but not Ermo. That is why that church is punishing him like this. Because he would not kneel to a man who thought he was God.

I took vases and glasses and whatever I could find that would break and threw them to the floor. Mamma was terrified of me then. She pleaded with me to calm down.

Finally, I asked her, what will they do with him? And that is when she told me if we did not claim Ermo and take him, they would bury him in the prison yard.

I wept uncontrollably until I knew the answer, because it was Ermo telling me what to do.

Why do you want me in a churchyard? He asked me. This life with all its corruption and dishonesty and greed is a prison. We tried, our little gruppo, to change it, but we could not, so let my bones lie in the prison yard. It is the truth of this life. We are all in a prison of our own making. And I knew he was right. I told this to Mamma. I grabbed my chest and told her he was there and would always be there, planted forever in my heart. I told her to let the prison bury him, and then I shut myself in my room.

I stopped caring for the children, only Bella, only having her on my breast, that is the only thing that let me know I was still alive. I know it was a luxury in a way, this breakdown, to shut out the world this way. I could do it because of Mamma and Aunt Abelia who took care of everything. So it was a luxury, to lose my mind. What would have happened to us if I did not have them?

Little at a time, I came back to myself. I washed. I combed my hair. I dressed. And finally I came to the table to sit with my family, my family as it was then, without Ermo, without Giù. The grief I had was as much as I could bear, no less. Each day that passed I could bear it more. I was able to endure. That is the best I could do, endure.

One day, three months, maybe more, after Ermo and Giù, a strange thing happened. We had a visitor. It was Silvio.

By then everyone from our group was gone. Many had been deported. It was too late for the brothers, but so many others went home to Italy. That was not a good thing, to be deported, but they were still alive, at least. The Sanchinis, Luigi —many others—were ordered to leave the country. But not Ella. She was in jail. And not Cino and not Silvio. They were free. Silvio had come to tell me things that I would scarcely believe.

I didn't want to let him in, but Mamma told me to. He may know things you should hear, she said. She and my aunt went into the boys' room and shut the door. Silvio and I sat on the sofa in the sitting room.

I don't want to disturb you in your grief, he began, but things are bothering me, things you should know. Things I have to get off my mind. He stopped to see if I would listen. I didn't say anything. I just looked at him and nodded, so he continued.

When the gruppo stopped meeting and became silent, didn't you wonder why I kept coming?

I answered Silvio immediately. It was because Cino was worried about us and was hiding, too, I said.

That was some hiding, he said, almost laughing.

I didn't like this attitude in Silvio, but it was true, what he was saying. I had often wondered about Cino. Ermo did, too, but he was our cousin. He was generous to us during our terrible time, I said to Silvio.

Generous, you might say, he said with a smirk on his face. He was raising issues of doubt. Then he said, maybe Cino was guilty.

I stopped him and stood up. If you have come to say bad things about our cousin, you can leave, I told him.

No, no, he said. Let me explain.

I waited, thinking it over, before I sat down and listened.

Silvio didn't say anything for a while. I think he was afraid I would chase him away. So when he began, he spoke slowly and chose his words carefully.

I know you never trusted me, dear Amalia. To you I was an errand boy for Cino, but who was I? Was I one of Cino's followers? Yes, you might say so, but more than that, we were all followers of Luigi. Then Silvio paused again. He took a deep breath and shook his head. No, he said. Let me start again.

Do you remember the day when Cino's place was crawling with police? When Cino's men all ran away? They never came back, because it wasn't just the police. Those beat cops never knew about us or cared. Who cared what the Italians were doing in their own neighborhoods? They didn't trust us or want anything to do with us. To them we didn't exist. No, it was the feds behind that raid. Because to them, we existed. Cino was being watched, and he knew it. Everyone in town knew Cino held meetings and talked about subversive things, you might say. And for a time there was nothing to be done about it. It was a free country. You could say what you wanted, but that changed. And you remember, Cino was arrested with the Sanchinis. And you know they were deported. So I ask you, why is Cino still here?

I didn't answer Silvio. Part of me wanted to make him stop. But I knew what was coming. In my heart, I did. And I finally realized it was time to face what I already knew. My hands were on my ears, and Silvio was waiting to see if this was my answer to his question. Without looking at him, I took my hands away.

Look, dear Amalia, he said, reaching for my hand, which I pulled away with such force, he shook in disbelief.

You may tell me what you have come to say, I told him, but don't ever touch me.

Mi dispiace. Perdonami. I will honor your wishes. Here is what I have to say.

When Cino was arrested, he was questioned by agents in Boston. But that was just for show.

I glared at him, not understanding what he was saying.

Don't be shocked, Amalia. You must have suspected. Why did Cino still have money when you had to close your shop? Who was paying to keep his open? Yes, he cared for you and Ermo, because he could, after his deal. Once the feds began to realize how active the New Britain cell was, they targeted Cino. They knew about his shop and his meetings, all with followers of Galleani. They knew all this long before his arrest.

When Silvio said these things, I was confused, because, yes, I had wondered about Cino, and so did Ermo, but we wouldn't let ourselves believe the worst. We were blinded. Not because he was family and we trusted him. Those things were true to a point, but when we were in trouble, we needed him. And that is why we pushed our doubts aside. Knowing Silvio was going to make me face the truth, with Ermo gone, was making me crazy again. But I had to listen.

Even when his shop was raided, and I called out the spy. All that was planned, Silvio said. It was important that no one in the gruppo began to doubt Cino's allegiance to the cause. When everyone was underground, Cino was taken away one night. The men who took him told Felice to keep quiet if she wanted to see him again. And she followed orders. No one even noticed he was gone because the gruppo was silent then.

The feds took Cino to Boston. And I can tell you, they were bad to him. I was there.

When Silvio said this, I couldn't catch my breath. He tried to offer help but remembered what I told him. I would die rather than let him help me. I coughed and gagged until Mamma came out of the bedroom to see if I was all right. I got up and rushed her back into the boys' room. I calmed down and Silvio tried to explain himself.

I have to tell you these things, Amalia. I don't know what you plan for your future, but you must know you will be watched for a long time, for years. They know you were the one who brought Erasmo in, more than Cino. Your husband joined the gruppo because of you.

Silvio was saying to my face the very thing I was afraid of. This traitor was breaking my already broken heart. I remained calm and nodded that I was all right. But I was not. I wanted to kill him.

He continued.

I was working with the Bureau from the beginning. I ingratiated myself with Cino. He learned that I was the real spy in Boston. After that he had to accept me, and I played the role of his errand boy. So I was there when we questioned him. He couldn't have water, couldn't use the toilet. They made him stay in a dark room alone for hours before they started on him, still in handcuffs, the whole time, like a criminal. He told them over and over he was a pacifist but didn't know anything about anarchists or Luigi Galleani. They knew better. They knew the names of everyone who had been to see Galleani when he was in New Britain. Of course, your name was on the list and also Erasmo's. They knew about every one of you. That is when things got very hard for your cousin. He had been under an agent's surveillance. George Lillard was his name.

I don't think Silvio realized how his words hit me, like a punch in the stomach. How bad could it have been for Cino, when it was Ermo and Giù who were dead? I let him keep talking.

You see, Silvio said, the feds next threatened Cino's wife and children. 'We will arrest Felice and take your children away to an orphanage, or if they don't speak English so good, we'll put them in a place for idiots.' That's what Lillard told him, and this made Cino crazy. Felice didn't know so much about her husband's work with the Galleanisti. He always told her he just had rights of free speech and that he was a patriot for a better country. The truth would kill her, he thought. She was a member of the church who volunteered to make immigrants adjust better. She was like an American. And the kids, Cino knew of kids who had been taken away. This was a tactic of the government. 'Tell us what we want to know, and you'll go home, a free man,' they told him. Then they took him to a solitary cell. 'You think about it,' they told him. He asked them many times, 'What do you want to know?' but they didn't say. The room had a heavy metal door. They slammed it shut and made him stay all night, no food or water.

The next morning, when they took him back to the room for more questions, there was coffee and donuts on the table. He said the smell was like heaven. The feds ate and drank but gave him nothing. 'So Cino,' they said, 'we have a problem and a solution.'

'We know what you do, and we know this Galleani is a very dangerous man, but right now our hands are tied. We arrest him, and he goes free. Why? We know the law behind us isn't strong enough yet. Too many sympathizers are making the rules. You live here because you didn't like your own country, and now you don't like this one. Well, we want to send you back, but we can't right now. So we have to send a message to all of you who don't know how good you have it. You have to know, by example, it's dangerous to threaten our way of life, with your bombs and speeches and pamphlets against the war, our government, against what we stand for in this country.'

There was much Cino could have said to this, but he held his tongue. He was very cautious, you see. He didn't know what they wanted from him. And then they told him.

'Give us someone, a name we can use.' Cino said nothing. This went on until all the coffee and donuts were gone. The two feds took turns taking breaks. Cino was tied to the chair. When they came back, the one in charge changed the questioning. 'Look, Cino,' he said. 'We know these people are your compadres, or whatever you call them, so for their sake you need to help us. Here's what we want. Give us a name of someone, anyone, who did something against the government, or someone you can get to do it, a deed, that's what you call it, right? When you commit an act of treason. Because that's what we call it.'

Cino could have had a discussion about this, but they had him, and all he could do was listen.

'It has to be a crime, not words in a speech on in a paper, something illegal,' he said. 'Give us the name and the deed, so we can make an example. Look, it won't be so bad. We'll arrest the guy, put him on trial, let the press know it's an anarchist who did it. Maybe he goes to jail for a while, maybe not, but that's it. Nothing more serious than that. You'd be doing your compadres a favor. We send the message, and we leave them and you alone then. Okay, think about it. In the meantime, you need to use the toilet?'

A policeman came in and took Cino away. When they brought him back in the room, there was more coffee and donuts on the table.

Silvio told me these things in such a way that I would understand why Cino did it. But he was wrong. I did not forgive Cino. I thought of Ella. I knew they did the same things to her. But she did not give anyone up for coffee and donuts. He was a weak man, Cino. I thought of how he made Erasmo transport the dynamite that would go to Ella that would lead to her arrest. It was clear that it was all connected and that it was Cino who did it. I sat still, not moving or looking at Silvio. Without making a sound, tears were rolling down my cheeks. He took a handkerchief from his pocket to give to me. I pushed it away and turned my head to wipe my face with my hands. I asked if he was through.

There's more I must tell you, he said. You can blame Cino for giving up Erasmo. But he did not do the rest. He told them about the dynamite but only that Erasmo had to deliver it to Youngstown. 'I don't know more than that' he said. 'We're not told everything, so we can't tell everything, to men like you.'

You have always wondered who I was, the man in shadows, I know what is said behind my back. The one doing Cino's bidding. Yes, it is true. I was Cino's man. And I was loyal. Until.

And then Silvio stopped, and my heart did too, I think because there was something more coming that would be more than I could take, and what would I do with this knowledge? I simply, then, held my breath. He had more to tell me, and I would hear it. I had no choice.

What Cino did, it would have ended there. Erasmo arrested, but not Giù, too. Not if it had ended there. It would have been what the fed said to Cino, an example, a jail sentence maybe, but when it involved Ella, then it got, much bigger. It involved Carlo, who was a fugitive. It tied the New Britain gruppo to the Milwaukee trial of the Galleanisti there. It opened the whole thing, the plan for revenge for the comrades in Milwaukee. It tied you to them. It revealed the New Britain gruppo as true Galleanisti, no longer harmless picnickers and singers who put on plays.

Now Silvio was shaking. He was soon to be beside himself. I was scared for him and for me. I kept looking back at the door to the boys' bedroom, where they were and my mother and aunt. I looked to be sure the door to our bedroom was closed and was relieved that it was and that Bella was sleeping quietly. I had a sense of what a desperate man might do. He was going to tell me things he could not take back, and then we would all be in danger. I begged him to stop.

You do not have to say more, I told him. This is enough.

No, he said. I must. I cannot tell a priest, but I can tell you. Don't be afraid, please, he said. Per favore, let me speak. And I did.

I was Cino's man. And I respected him, and I came to believe his followers in Kensington and all of you in your gruppo, I came to see you had your reasons. There was so much wrong, so much hatred against those not in power and so much corruption in those who had it. But I was lost then. Nowhere to turn. I was not one of you from the beginning. I was a plant, a snitch, from the beginning. An Italian by birth with a record, no hope, and the threat of prison over my head, I was a natural to spy and snitch. And I did. Cino accepted me immediately, not knowing, not suspecting. First, I came to meetings, then I started running errands, a package here, a message there. He came to trust me. All the while I was reporting back to the Bureau what was happening. The feds knew about Erasmo, but they needed Cino to break, to tell his contacts there was danger. To sow fear, that was what they were after. Scared targets get stupid. They make mistakes. They wanted to make chaos among the Galleanisti, and this was a way to do it. Luigi and the Sanchinis were prime targets, and Erasmo was brought into a larger plot, without knowing it.

Silvio stopped and looked at me. I was stone. He continued.

That porter on Ella's train never would have known to get

her out of her cabin so he could search her valise if not for me. He never would have found the dynamite, if not for me. I was the one who told the feds at the Bureau to watch that train. I knew the plan, and I knew it because Cino knew it, and he trusted me. But he was not the one to give everyone up. I was.

How much more of Silvio's confession could I take? If all this was true, what went so terribly wrong that Ermo and Giù had to die? I took a deep breath and asked.

Dear Amalia. The worst is yet to be said. By then there was a fever, worse than the terrible Spanish flu. These men had become infected with hatred, with fear. They had secret agents everywhere telling stories of treachery and sedition. They wanted blood, the blood of anarchists and they had Erasmo and Giuseppe, like birds in their rifle sights, because of what Cino gave them, Erasmo and the dynamite.

He crumbled then. His head in his hands. Did he want my sympathy, my forgiveness? I could not give it. But no, that wasn't it. He just had to say it, to tell someone. That night I was his priest. My sofa, his confessional. Perdonami, over and over he said it. With no thought of how his words cut me to shreds.

He stood to leave. But he was not through. There was innocent blood on his hands that he could not bear, and so he said to me before he left ...

The two witnesses, the ones who saw two men rushing for a waiting car, the ones the judge said didn't change anything, and so there was no retrial. These two men, they are the reason Giù was also arrested. These two men, they were the ones who did it. They killed Palmese. They were agents. One of them had been spying on Cino. George Lillard, the one who was there when Cino was being interrogated. The whole thing was out of Cino's control. He never meant it to go this far. By this time, it wasn't about sending a simple message anymore. It was about an out-of-whack idea of American justice when the laws were too weak. You see, don't you? When your husband and his brother were held up as examples of what could happen to anarchists, it was before the law changed. After the law changed to deport anarchists, it was too late. They were already tried and convicted for a murder they didn't commit, and there was no one to make it right. Not me, not Cino. We were too weak and too doomed to say anything. *La pace tra gli oppressi, la guerra agli oppressor.* You remember these words by our poet? I believe them. Look what I have done. Try to forgive us.

And then Silvio left. I never said a word to him. I couldn't. I would never forget what he told me. Forgiveness was a word not in my vocabulary. Forgiveness, after this? No. Those words, *La pace tra gli oppressi, la guerra agli oppressor.* They were by Pietro Gori, our poet, not Silvio's, no matter how he tried to say he became one of us. Gori wrote those words in prison. Peace to the oppressed. War to the oppressor. We believed these words. Look what has become of them.

Here is the last thing I have to tell you. The next day Cino came to see us. I wouldn't come out from our bedroom, mine and Ermo's. Cino was used to my saying no to his visits because I was so sick after what happened. But he insisted it was urgent. My mother let him in. Silvio is dead he told her. He was found in his car with a bullet in his head. He was tormented. He did it to himself.

It still hurts, after all these years, to remember these things. After this, you will come to see me, but we will never speak of these times again.

19

CODA

Carinola, Italy
June 27, 2000

B ut there was more Amalia would tell me when I next saw
her that year of my visits, when I had been so eager to
learn about my great uncles. In the afternoons we spent
together I had grown to care about all them, the anarchists of
New Britain. But more than anyone else, I came to care deeply
about Amalia, her story, how she had endured such tragedy.

I saw her again in late September 1995. We met in the
shade of the large oak in her backyard. She smiled when she
saw me, that smile, of two truths, yes and no, yes to enduring,
no to suffering; yes to resistance, no to injustice. It was true, she
was still resisting. She may have left the violence of Galleani's
Deed behind, but not the Idea. That beautiful possibility
remained in her, even if she knew the odds were impossible to
beat.

Bella brought us iced tea and sat with us in one of the three
green metal lawn chairs spaced under the tree. "My parents

had those same chairs when we lived in Miami," I said. "Like tulip petals."

I told Amalia she looked refreshed. Bella said it was true. Her mother had been much improved since my visits. And she was happy to see me again. Bella left us then, with a smile so different from her mother's, in a word, resigned. I didn't know her well; she always left us to our private talks, intervening only to ask if we needed anything. But I had my story about her, simply that she had foregone a life of her own to care for her mother, to always be near the woman who had endured such loss. Regardless of my conclusions about her, it was true that Bella had never married or had children of her own. After she left us, Amalia and I continued our visit.

"I think I feel better because I see how much I didn't forget. I've been saying for years, the past is dead. Let it be. But that wasn't true for me. Even though Cino has been dead for years now, I never forgave him. We continued to act as though we were a family. There were many times he joined us when we had family visitors, like the times when Francesco and Marianne came with the boys and their young daughter, Josephine. We talked of many things, but we never spoke of those days.

"I think Cino died knowing Silvio told me everything. I was very cold to him after the deaths of Ermo and Giù. You know, Cino became a big leader in town. A community leader and a churchman. Oh yes, no one ever mentioned the word anarchy again. I never went back to the church. My poor mamma and sweet zietta, Aunt Abelia, worried about my soul. They managed to get Bella confirmed. She still goes to mass, but not me."

I had nothing to say to this, except to remember that my mother and father saw to it that my sister and I received communion and were confirmed, but they never went with us to mass.

"After our talks," Amalia continued, "I came to see what Silvio was trying to tell me. They were weak, Cino and him, yes, but I came to see that it is very hard for a man, or a woman, to live up to beliefs that are beyond them."

I asked her what she meant, exactly, and she said, simply, "We're human, not gods. We cannot fix our faults. Oh yes, we can lose weight, stop smoking, but I'm talking about the basic fault, human nature. That we can't fix. Maybe someday, but not now."

I took this to mean she still believed the anarchist ideal could still be achieved in some distant future.

"In the meantime, we live with it."

Then she said something unlike her.

"I know now that living with it means not forgetting. It means accepting."

Most of the ideas she had expressed in our talks had been about anarchism, the ideal and the shattering of it, but this was more philosophic. She was apparently coming to terms with a lifetime of old wounds. If she was finding comfort, that was the important thing. I still didn't know what to do with all I had learned. I too had old wounds now, not mortal, but the story I had heard from her over the weeks and months had filled me with regret, a feeling I didn't know how to resolve. I longed for one more conversation with my father. I wanted to comfort him, and him, me. There was so much he knew and could have told me. I was too busy with my own life when he might have welcomed my questions. I was grieving this lost opportunity.

Amalia and I sipped our tea. A fresh breeze came up, hinting for a moment of cooler days ahead. A single leaf, still green, fell by our feet.

"You know," she said, "I did see Ella again."

I put my glass on the round metal table between us and listened.

"She went to prison, I think I told you. Her trial was at the same time as Ermo and Giù's, in October of 1918. In November, she was sent to prison in Missouri. She had connections there, famous ones, you know, Emma Goldman and Kate Richards O'Hare. Maybe the O'Hare woman wasn't as well known as Goldman, but she was a labor activist. It's an interesting story.

"After Ermo and Giù were gone, Ella came to see me. I was still on Cherry Street. Charley helped me change the house around. We made it into a boarding house, and I took in boarders. That's how we survived, the boys and me and Bella. I did that for a long time, until I moved here to be with Bella.

"When Ella came that day, we sat on the stoop. It was in the summer, nice, like today. We were drinking sodas from bottles and had our shoes off. We had our legs stretched out and our skirts hiked up, taking in the sun, like we were at the beach. I'm sure the neighbors saw, peeping at us through their curtains. It would have been a scandal, but that's what Ella was like, a free spirit, always. She never changed. We had a good, long visit.

"Emma and Kate doted on her," she told me. "They couldn't believe a girl so young could be so committed to our cause and be so brave. Even when she was under arrest and they tried to scare and intimidate her, she never cracked, and Emma and Kate adored her for her strength."

Amalia paused and smiled to herself remembering her friend. Not all her memories brought heartache.

"Ella loved telling that story," she continued, "about how they were the three darlings of the prison. All the women looked up to them, and they were kind to the others. They tried to be helpful, to write letters for them and such things. Ella told me that Emma and Kate couldn't believe how smart she was, that this poor immigrant Italian girl who had been through so much was so smart.

'They should've known you, Amalia,' she said to me. 'You were as smart as I was. We were something in our gruppo, weren't we?'

"She told me the one who helped the most to get her out of prison was Kate's husband, Frank. He got her out before her sentence was up. He was a powerful man and had connections in high places even though he was for labor and the rights of workers.

"While we were outside on the stoop drinking our sodas, she said she was thinking of marrying again. She did, too, not long after. But that day, we were just two modern women. It did me good to see her. We talked about the old days and the gruppo. She was still in touch with some and had met other new ones committed to our cause. She knew Sacco and Vanzetti. But this was before that case. She told me in a letter a year later, after their arrest, that the feds got cocky after Erasmo and Giuseppe. They thought they could get away with it again, but she didn't think so. She thought Sacco and Vanzetti would go free because of all the publicity, all the famous people on their side. I didn't want to tell her, but I knew, even then how it would turn out. My whole family knew what the government could do when what they wanted had nothing to do with justice.

"But what I remember most about that day was something she said about the Galleanisti. 'They used us, Lia,' she said. 'What they wanted was more important than each one of us. The cause was greater, but what did it mean, then, if human life wasn't the most important thing? Weren't we fighting for better lives?'

"We didn't have any answers, she and I, but I always remembered that. She was used and paid for it. Ermo and Giù were used, and paid with their lives. I gave it all up, but she stayed true to the Beautiful Idea just the same."

Amalia and I talked well into the afternoon. Before I left I asked what had become of Aldo and Nino. Maybe I shouldn't have, because I knew they were dead, but I was hoping she would tell me they had lived happy lives.

"They had their ups and downs, like everyone," she said. But there was a sudden sadness in her voice. I thought it was a mistake, asking, but she wanted to talk.

"You should know this," she said, "because this is the truth about what they did to us. Aldo and Nino finished school, had jobs, had wives and families, both of them. But there was always sadness in them. They lived knowing something terrible had happened. Maybe I should have talked about it more, but I thought it was best to let it alone, let them, Ermo and Giù, stay buried. Maybe nothing would have helped. In the end, though, it mattered that my sons didn't have their father to help them grow up. They died before me, both sick. And I know why, because something like this, like what happened to us, it leaves its mark. It didn't just happen to Ermo and Giù. It happened to all of us. Some survive it better than others. But no one escapes. That's what I've learned."

And then, it spite of all she had told me, she smiled. She stood up and opened her arms to me. We hugged for a long time. I stifled my tears. She did not cry.

After my visit with Amalia, I was confused, angry at what my government had done, and sad for the toll it had exacted. And I was happy, too, to see Amalia stronger than she had been in months. My own feelings were a tangled web. I missed my father. That missed opportunity, to talk, to comfort him, for him to share this part of his life with me.

When I left Amalia that day, I was already looking forward to my next visit. We agreed I would come again as long as the weather was nice, so we could sit outside under the tree. Amalia told me she was dreading winter. "I'm not sure I want to see another one," she said, laughing, the last time I saw her.

When the day of our next visit was nearing, Bella called. My pounding heart told me what she would say. "Mamma died in her sleep."

"I'm so sorry, I said."

"You loved her. She loved you, too."

I wanted to say more but instead, I cried.

"She was holding the handkerchief my father gave her. She never stopped loving him."

Bella and I cried together then before hanging up. I wondered what would happen to her now.

The day of Amalia's funeral was the last nice day before an early snowstorm. I continue to visit her at Fairview, a nonsectarian cemetery in New Britain. Occasionally I talk to Bella. She still lives in their house.

* * *

When Amalia died, I wasn't through with the story. I couldn't be. I continued my research to see what more I could uncover. Mostly what I found confirmed everything she ever told me.

I found a retrospective article that appeared in the *Hartford Courant*, July 3, 1921. After the war and the anti-immigrant hysteria of the Red Scare had died down, Governor Holcomb, Lucien F. Burpee (the judge in Erasmo and Giuseppe's case), and agents of the Bureau of Investigation were lauded in this article for their cooperative work in ferreting out enemy aliens and for their relentless pursuit of draft dodgers and slackers. The article explains how the American Protective League was formed, as part of the Bureau of Investigation under the United States Department of Justice.

Governor Holcomb had the authority to appoint the executive officers of the league in Connecticut, and he, of course, appointed Burpee. In turn, his appointees served under the direction of George W. Lillard from Justice. This is the agent who first filed a Bureau report saying that Ella's husband, Augusto Segata, was friends with Cino when he was first under suspicion for anarchist meetings in Kensington. Lillard is portrayed as quiet and self-effacing while at the same time being wily and effective (the stereotype of the feds in the early days, when they were admired as sort of the prototypal American hero).

But tucked in the article is a description that caused my arms to tingle. He is described as "Little Chief Lillard," stockily built—the same description as one of the men identified by eyewitnesses in my uncles' case. These witnesses testified that the men seen leaving the vicinity of the crime did not match my uncles' descriptions. Neither Erasmo nor Giuseppe was stocky. Giù was gaunt and thin. The article also describes in great detail how one unnamed agent was awakened in the middle of the night and told to come to the office building in Hartford in forty minutes with a car. When he arrived, another agent piled in and the car took off, speeding south. Two men in suits, one stockily built, speeding toward New Britain.

Lillard, it turns out, was let go in July of 1919, amid speculation that his departure was politically motivated. The implication is that Lillard may have been too zealous in the execution of his duties. *The Courant*, reporting on his removal, notes that "although approximately sixty-five percent of the munitions manufactured in the country were made in Connecticut, the state was entirely free from disturbance during the war activities," implying that Lillard, was largely responsible. The article then adds that during this time, Lillard was associated with Lucien Burpee, whose name by then is all but synonymous with tough-minded pursuit of enemy aliens and, of course, anarchists.

The league described later in the article provided what was hailed as "eyes and ears," with investigators whose duty it was to be aware of "suspicious circumstances and seditious talk" and then to report such activity to ensure whatever action might be considered necessary. That article pulls back the curtain on a homegrown secret surveillance and justice system operating outside of established law enforcement, with the blessing of the Bureau of Investigation. Lillard may have been too zealous, but he gets credit in the press for keeping Connecticut safe.

Erasmo and Giuseppe's trial, during the heat of the Red Scare, took place at a time of intense hostility toward immigrants. The prosecuting attorney in the case played on the fears of the jury against these men with "their arsenals," and the judge led a state-sponsored secret service against perceived seditionists. It's hard to imagine the verdict going any other way. When the verdict of guilty was returned, many (the press included) were surprised based on the weaknesses in the case. It is easy to conclude that, given this climate, the two men had been convicted because of their foreign birth and radical beliefs, no matter how weak the evidence against may have been.

In spite of new evidence produced on appeal, the attitudes of the authorities had become so rigidly set against the defendants that they turned a deaf ear to contrary views. At the eleventh hour, Holcomb denied the plea for a last-minute pardon. And so they died, but not necessarily for the crime for which they were convicted. I came to fully believe they died for those "anarchistic tendencies" the press referred to.

Their fate was truly sealed on June 9, 1919, before this last-ditch effort with the governor, when the Board of Pardons heard the brothers' plea to have their death sentence commuted to life in prison. According to another article I found in *the Hartford Courant*, the brothers' new counsel, Judge Tuttle and attorney, Salvator D'Esopo, brought the case for commutation forward. They argued on the flimsiness of the circumstantial case, the insufficient evidence, the weak motive, and the ignored eyewitness testimony. The state's position, as set forth by Hugh Alcorn (the prosecuting attorney during the trial), argued that the defense had never before questioned the evidence and that the court had heard before the testimony that two men had been seen leaving the vicinity of the murder. The *Courant* then quotes Alcorn: "As both are anarchists," according to the state's attorney, the state did not require "a decided motive for the killing." Here is the state's attorney blatantly admitting that the brothers are to be executed for their political beliefs, although no charges for sedition or other illegal activity had ever been brought against them, and that because they are anarchists, the state has no burden to produce a motive for the crime for murder for which they were arrested and tried. The Board of Pardons ruled against the brothers. The death sentence was upheld. Erasmo knew it when he wrote to the governor, when he declared he and his brother "were all framed up."

* * *

With this knowledge and Amalia's recent death still weighing on me, I was desperate to visit my father's hometown of Saviano, in the district of San Terma. I was grasping at straws, hoping to find some link to the brothers in their hometown, their birthplace, and my father's. My husband and I planned a trip to Italy for the following year. The first stop was Naples and a hotel on the lungomare, looking across the bay to Vesuvius. (Little did I know then that we would be returning often, to a villa not far from Saviano, in Carinola, the hometown of my grandmother, Marianne. It had been her family's property when she was a baby. When it came on the market, my husband and I bought it.)

The water in the Bay of Naples sparkles as though it is electric. No matter what time of day, the boys of Naples dive from the rocks and then float on their backs in the sun. It is easy for me to know why my father, when he spoke of it at all, spoke of this land with affection. I feel close to my father when I'm there, and closer yet in Saviano.

On that trip in '96, in my father's hometown, we were able to locate records from the town hall, my father's birth certificate and my grandparents' marriage certificate. We were lucky to find these, the town clerk told us. Many civil and church records were destroyed during the war. We were not so lucky finding records for my great grandparents. No luck finding Nicoletta, or her sons, other than my grandfather's marriage certificate, no Erasmo or Giuseppe, not at the town hall or at the church, San Erasmo. Everywhere I turned, I looked for signs, my great grandmother's garden, her orange trees. I looked for the house where my father may have been born, the fountain where children were sent to fetch water for their mothers. My father mentioned this chore and the fountain in Saviano. No luck, but we did see more than one house with the name Perretta. It seems in Saviano, this is a fairly common name.

We were walking through town in the afternoon when the shops were closed and the clinking of silverware could be heard from the houses. At one Perretta address, we randomly rang the doorbell and soon someone came out to the balcony. My husband called up to him, "Siamo parenti. Mia moglie è Perretta." We offered no proof of a family relationship, but the man on the balcony waved us up. Climbing the stairs, I noticed the garden. There was an orange tree. Our host introduced himself as Salvatore.

"Call me Sal," he said in careful English.

We were promptly invited to lunch with him, his wife, and their two adult children. We told them of our mission, to find relatives of my great uncles. They were very sympathetic. His wife Angela said it was a sad story, not like the America of everyone's dream. Maybe they never should have left, she said. Maybe.

After broiled chicken, salad, wine, and cake for dessert, Sal brought out the family album. We exchanged stories of relatives, those still in Italy and those in America, but soon we had to admit defeat. We were no doubt relatives but very distant, many times removed. They were wonderfully gracious to us. After expressing our gratitude, "grazie molte, grazie mille," we said our goodbyes. But before leaving, I turned and asked, "Dov'è la fontana?" Our host looked at me quizzically, my Italian being rudimentary. My husband explained.

Sal answered, "È qui," he said, gesturing across the street. "Grazie ancora," I said, as I rushed down the stairs.

The fountain was an iron hand pump, easy to miss. I pumped the handle and cupped my hands in the water and then washed my face and rubbed my wet hands around my neck. I dried off in the sun as we walked back to the car.

Maybe it was a sign, maybe Erasmo and Giuseppe were telling me to let them rest. The next morning, I couldn't turn my head. My stiff neck lasted all day. I was reminded of Amalia. She would never mistake a romantic notion such as finding my father's fountain for some mystical connection. Finding my father's fountain did not give meaning to the hunt for Perrettas in Saviano. I had found no answers.

* * *

After Naples, we decided to go to Ravello, a town my husband and I had fallen in love with years earlier on a different trip. After the same hairpin curves, the Mediterranean below, nothing but a battered guardrail between us and eternity, we came to the magic of the place, with its farms of delicate terraces perched wherever available earth allows, yielding crops of tomatoes, lettuces, and an array of summer vegetables, spilling over the edges of the narrow space. The air was filled with the aroma of basil and oregano and the occasional sweetness of lavender.

Overwhelmed with the beauty of this country, I thought of Angela and her words, "Maybe they should never have left." Then I remembered my stiff neck. No easy, romantic notions.

It was no mistake we were there in late June. It was my way of honoring an anniversary. I rose early in the morning of the twenty-eighth. I quietly left the bedroom and in the bathroom, I pushed open the shutters of the window. The moon was still casting its light on the mountain in the distance. Far off, I heard barking, perhaps of the wild dogs we'd been warned about in the restaurant the night before.

I imagined a young Amalia in the darkened bedroom, the door shut. On the other side her mother and aunt and my grandmother are watching the children. My grandfather is there and Cino, his brother. My father, Michele, and his brother, Antonio, are playing with their cousins on the floor. They are told silenzio if they become too loud. The adults wipe their eyes from time to time, quieting their own sorrow while listening for any call for comfort, but Amalia is beyond comfort, beyond remedy. She lies curled on top of their bed, hers and Erasmo's. The only movement she makes is in her hands, as she wrings Erasmo's handkerchief, yellow, trimmed in lace. From time to time she mumbles imprecations against the land that is taking her life from her, taking her breath, her heart, her soul. I hear her curses, as she described them, on the lawyers, the judge, the jury. She calls on special powers, granted to her by the enormity of her affliction, and casts a most malignant curse on his Excellency, the Honorable Governor Holcomb, whose silence foretold the brothers' doom.

This story of my family is old and it is new. Their grief lives on in us.

I hear the low, mournful tolling of bells somewhere in the distance, six in all.

What the study could not teach—what the preaching could not accomplish—is accomplished, is it not? Whitman's words come to me in this foreign land that is my home. *Suspend here and everywhere, eternal float of solution!*

The mystery remains suspended. Those who came before us keep their secrets permanently planted within us. Be at peace; be at peace, I pray. Great or small, we furnish our parts toward eternity; we furnish our parts.

ACKNOWLEDGMENTS

My thanks to Arlene Palmer, now retired, from the New Britain Public Library, for directing me to articles in the *New Britain Herald* before digitized newspapers. More recently, thanks go to Emily Mulvey at the library for her help in locating archival maps of New Britain. Similarly, Amy Martin, Research Center Assistant at the Connecticut Historical Society and Additionally, thanks to Maureen D. Heher, historical research specialist, Hartford History Center, at the Hartford Public Library, who located an early twentieth century *Hartford Courant* newspaper article about the workings of the Hartford courts, along with interior sketches of the courtrooms.

Finally, books that have provided invaluable background:

Paul Avrich's *Anarchist Voices: An Oral History of Anarchism in America.*
Bruce Frazier's unpublished dissertation, *Yankee's at War: Social Mobilization on the Connecticut Homefront, 1917–1918,* Columbia University.
Emma Goldman's Autobiography, *Living My Life.*
Kate Richards O'Hare's *In Prison* and *Selected Writings and Speeches,* edited by Philp S. Foner and Sally M. Miller.

Special thanks to publisher, Lisa Kastner, whose commitment to giving voice to stories that otherwise would not be told is both bold and admirable; to my editor, A.E. Williams, for wise and astute observations that made this book better; to Lidia Sophia Townsley, who graciously scrutinized my Italian, and to product manager, Evangeline Estropia. Her warmth and professionalism are a rare and appreciated combination. Also, thanks to my husband, Steve, first and last reader, whose patience and support are beyond measure. Finally, a note of appreciation to my sons, Jerry and Chris, whose early encouragement spurred me on.

My sincere thanks to all.

Running Wild Press publishes stories that cross genres with great stories and writing. RIZE publishes great genre stories written by people of color and by authors who identify with other marginalized groups. Our team consists of:

Lisa Diane Kastner, Founder and Executive Editor
Cody Sisco, Acquisitions Editor, RIZE
Benjamin White, Acquisition Editor, Running Wild
Peter A. Wright, Acquisition Editor, Running Wild
Resa Alboher, Editor
Angela Andrews, Editor
Sandra Bush, Editor
Ashley Crantas, Editor
Rebecca Dimyan, Editor
Abigail Efird, Editor
Aimee Hardy, Editor
Henry L. Herz, Editor
Cecilia Kennedy, Editor
Barbara Lockwood, Editor
Scott Schultz, Editor

Evangeline Estropia, Product Manager
Kimberly Ligutan, Product Manager
Lara Macaione, Marketing Director
Joelle Mitchell, Licensing and Strategy Lead
Pulp Art Studios, Cover Design
Standout Books, Interior Design
Polgarus Studios, Interior Design

Learn more about us and our stories at www. runningwildpress.com

Loved this story and want more? Follow us at www.runningwildpress.com, www.facebook.com/runningwildpress, on Twitter @lisadkastner @RunWildBooks